A CHESTNUT HILLS SMALL-TOWN ROMANCE

Lessons in Control

MARIA ROSEWOOD

Contents

For my village.

prologue

daisy

LEANING OVER THE PINK motel sink, I stared into the water spot-stained mirror and widened my eyes to apply a coat of blue mascara. I decided long ago, if I couldn't control my circumstances, I sure a shell could at least control looking bad ass.

"Mom! Are you up?" I called into the small room behind me. Mom moaned from the second queen sized bed in response. "We need to leave; school starts in fifteen minutes!"

Walking into the shared living space, I took in my mom still laying sprawled across her bed. Dressed in jean shorts and T-shirt from the day before, a mini bottle of vodka rested on the pillow next to her.

Rolling my eyes at the familiar sight, I scrounged for something quick and easy to eat. *I guess I'll have to walk to school.* Great, it was my first day at yet another new school and I was already late. Even though it was my fifth high school, I still wanted to be on time. Secretly, I hoped to make at least one friend in the new town.

If the prospect of making a new friend wasn't enough to get my ass out the door, the thought of my near future was. In two glorious months, I would turn eighteen at the same time I was scheduled to graduate. Both worked together to create a big bright light at the end of my motel laden tunnel.

Then, I could walk away and never look back.

Luckily, the walk to school was easy. The cracked sidewalk guided the path straight to the parking lot. Spring was just beginning to break, and the light morning breeze was a welcoming comfort.

Coming up into the parking lot, I could hear the bell ring throughout the parked cars. Save for the surrounding cars, I was alone. Yep, I was late. Swearing, I broke into a light jog.

The vast and awkwardly shaped building became more complicated, with the halls branching in every direction. Each hall housed more and more classrooms. Finally, I found my way to Room 238 *History, Mrs. Larkin.* A large clock at the end of the hallway loomed over me, showing that I was eleven minutes late. Gingerly, I opened the heavy door.

"Hello." an older woman in a matching lime green pantsuit stood at the whiteboard, a marker in hand. "Can I help you?"

My plans of entering unseen were squashed at being called out and I awkwardly giggled, closing the door behind me.

"Hi, I'm new. Daisy Bloom?"

"Oh yes, I was expecting you," the woman pursed her lips, glancing at the clock above her desk, "*eleven* minutes ago."

Heat creeped up my cheeks. Scanning the room, I took in all the unfamiliar faces, hoping for a sympathetic one. Instead, I found about twenty dead-pan teens looking at me.

"There's an empty desk in the back. Please take a seat—and take care to be *on time* tomorrow."

Shyly apologizing and agreeing, I held my cheetah print tote bag close to me as I wove through the organized desks.

"Word has it, Mrs. Larkin has never smiled. Like ever. That's why her face looks like it's a wax mask," a low voice murmured behind me.

Rather than risking getting caught fraternizing during class and turning to see who threw me a life raft, I leaned back and spoke out of the side of my mouth.

"She vaguely reminds me of a middle school teacher I had that was rumored to eat chalk—I see no chalk around. Coincidence?"

The mystery guy behind me laughed, earning us both a pointed look. Pinching my lips together, I sat forward and did my best to remain quiet for the rest of the class. Two glorious months stood between me and my high school diploma. Switching schools more than once a year made it difficult to keep up with the academic standards in each district, so I had had to adapt. Each class required my full attention.

The bell set the room of students in motion, everyone knowing their next destination but me. Checking my schedule, I saw a pair of black sneakers behind the sheet of paper.

"Where are you headed next, new girl?"

I looked up, thankful for a potential friend. "Mr. Kates?"

"Ah yes, the hardest statistics teacher on this side of Maryland...I'll show you the way," he waited for me as I folded my schedule back up, tucking it away into my bag.

My new friend introduced himself as Iggy. According to him, it was because he was the only kid lucky enough to have a pet iguana. According to his friends I met at lunch, it was because he looked eerily similar to his pet iguana. Either way, I was happy to have made acquaintances on the first day.

The happiness of the day slipped away as I took in the empty, musty motel room.

Being alone wasn't the issue, not having anything to eat other than a Honey Bun was. Ignoring my rumbling belly, I finished my homework in an hour flat and watched the Home and Garden channel until I fell asleep. Daydreaming of having my own home one day, my own space, kept the hunger at bay and lulled me to sleep.

A weight on the edge of the bed pulled me from my sleep. Through the darkness of the room lit by the still playing television, a warm sour breath filled my space.

"Mom?" Through my grogginess, the smell of alcohol gave my mom's presence away.

Humming, mom moved up behind me, wrapping an arm around my waist. I felt her speak into my hair, her words slurred.

"Curl kicked out his girl-f-f-friend, we mov-e in tomor-row. I'm sorry I wasn' homme. I lo-ove youu, Daizy Ma-ae."

I rolled my eyes at the statement. I didn't know who the hell Curl, or who I assumed was actually Carl, was, but I hoped that he at least had a stocked pantry.

This time to lull myself back to sleep, I silently recited to myself, *two more months, two more months.*

one

daisy

"Daisy?" a young female voice called from the front of my small-town pottery and ceramics studio and shop.

Distracted by delicately using a wire to loosen my latest clay creation from the pottery wheel, I opted for biting my bottom lip over responding.

"Ah, I knew you'd be back here," Calley, one of my high school part-time employees, entered the back room with a smile. "Just wanted to let you know I'm here for my shift...what is that?"

Carefully setting the vase down to dry, I tilted my head to observe my artwork. "A vase! Inspired by a formation of birds. It's cool, right?"

It was a wonder the tower of clay was still standing. Varying unique shaped bowls were precariously stacked on top of each other, slightly resembling a flock of birds. If you squinted...and bent your neck at a ninety-degree angle.

The abstract piece was a perfect depiction of my art. All my art required a little internal weirdness to understand. Creating these funky pieces was a passion of mine, along with pastries, ice cream, Jersey Shore—the reality TV show, not the location—and huge and equally fluffy dogs.

"Totally," Calley bobbed her head with an unconvincing sigh. "I'm gonna set up for the pottery painting class." She hiked her thumb with a chipped purple nail over her shoulder to the main studio area.

"Thanks." I swiped a hand across my forehead. "I'm just going to tidy up before heading out. Need anything?"

Being my own boss was cool. Liberating, even. Being someone else's boss was...awkward. I enjoyed having control and being a nice person. But being a boss meant I had to let go a little, and sometimes even had to be not so nice.

"Nope," the teen popped her gum, "have fun!" Turning to leave, she did a three-sixty and faced me again with a wince. "So sorry, Daisy. I just remembered there was something I meant to tell you. I'm going to have to call-out for Tuesday. I forgot I have tennis practice."

Ah man. I was going to have to be not-nice-boss-lady. I cleared my throat. My usual badass self-retreated inward, and I took a deep breath, coaxing it to come forward. "Calley, you have to let me know these things in advance. If Liam can't cover, I'm going to have to find extra help somewhere."

"I know, I know. I'm sorry," Calley cringed, putting up her hands in defense. "I'll get you my tennis schedule." With a wiggle of her fingers over her shoulder, she was gone.

"Sooner rather than later!" I called after her. Heaven help Calley's parents. Or any parents of teenagers, for that matter.

The late spring heat was creeping in and it was a perfect evening for rolling down the windows, blasting music, and letting my left hand hang out the window .Bertha, my big black SUV, was a prize possession. After my first successful year of running Slay & Clay, I treated myself to a new ride. I *needed* something big to carry all my creations to craft shows. I *wanted* something sexy because why the hell not?

It took me a few years to figure it out, but I'd been the proud owner of the local pottery shop and studio for six years. After stumbling on this quaint town, looking for nothing more than somewhere safe and away from my past, I settled in, making it my home.

At eighteen, I started with a room in a rooming house, a beat-up bike I got from a yard sale for thirty bucks, and a part-time job at the local ice cream shop, Loop & Scoop. The freedom, Uncle Ernie, my neighbor slash fellow housemate, and my best friend, Ellie, made my life pretty kick-ass. Some people may turn their noses up at the way I lived, but I'd be willing to bet they'd never listened to Uncle Ernie's stories of fishing in the Everglades while they ate ice cream at nine a.m. next to their best friend.

Six years later, I put a down payment on a little brick shop in the middle of downtown. What once was a secondhand bookstore was now my successful pottery shop and studio with an upper-level apartment. A year later, after becoming the hot spot for crafty date nights and the occasional senior center field trip, bing, bang, boom, I splurged on Bertha.

Whipping into a spot outside Ellie's apartment, I applied another coat of lip gloss before hopping out. After a fateful evening at our part-time jobs at Loop &Scoop, Ellie and I had been best friends ever since. We were each other's family.

Growing up an only child, and moving around a lot, I'd always yearned for genuine friendships. The kind I saw in movies and read about in books. I'd always wanted my own *Sisterhood of the Traveling Pants*. So, when Ellie and I clicked, I knew I'd found my girl. My ride or die.

What started as two girls just getting by, avoiding their bosses creepy ass son, turned into two girls thriving and paving their own way.

Using my best friend's spare key, I let myself in.

Sprawled out on her bed, I scrolled through Dately, the hot, new dating app, while I waited for her to change into a new top. Like hell I'd ever let her wear her cheating ex-boyfriend's shirt out in public.

Who are the top contenders tonight? Swipe, swipe, swipe. Oh, nice forearms. Swipe.

Though Chestnut Hills was a small-town community, it was a suburb of Philadelphia, which lent itself to an influx of visitors over the weekend. Especially when our town's celebrity band, the Assets, was playing. That meant the selection of men was always revolving, especially on nights like these.

"Whatcha' doin?" The bed dipped at the added weight as Ellie plopped next to me, leaning over my shoulder to watch me swipe.

"Checking out tonight's menu," I laughed nonchalantly; I was aware of what I sounded like, and I didn't care. As an adult, I was finally in a place to control my life. I had a successful business, fulfilling art hobby and career, and my own home. In the middle of being busy with all that, I liked to spend the night with a hunk-a-hunk every now and then.

One thing was for certain, though—no relationships. Relationships meant a boyfriend, and boyfriends are people, and people are uncontrollable. No, thankyou. No, sir. Not for me.

Instead, I liked to indulge in getting my rocks off, being told I was pretty, then being on my own again the next day.

"You're ridiculous," Ellie laughed, nudging my shoulder.

"I'm what you call 'playing the field.' Something you yourself should be doing."

For weeks, I'd been trying to get Ellie on the apps. After her ex cheated, she'd been down in the dumps. I don't blame her at all; it was pretty shitty how it happened. Her neighbors walked in on her ex doing it with the leasing office manager, and one of those neighbors was an absolute tatted stud who was hopelessly in love with her. Too dense to see her self-worth though, she struggled with dating, or even catching onto Theo's desperate chase for her.

"So, according to you, should I be playing the field, or pursuing Theo? I'm just a little confused about you inviting him out tonight, but also trying to get me on Dately, *again*." Ellie raised her eyebrows at me.

"Listen, I'm just trying to show you what's out there. Shane was an absolute dick, but he was not the end all be all. You deserve so much more, something good." I squeezed her hand and laid my head on her shoulder. "Theo can give you that, but if you're too stubborn to recognize that for whatever reason, then at least put yourself out there. See what's possible."

"Daze, I appreciate that. I do, but I'm still not there. I'm not willing to get hurt again, especially not by Theo."

I scoffed. "The man loves you, but whatever helps you sleep at night." A pillow hit the back of my head, immediately followed by Ellie's laughter.

My phone vibrated from the floor where it landed when I was attacked by downy softness. From my spot on the bed, I could see it was a text as a banner appeared across the lit screen.

"I'll get it," Ellie jumped off the bed to retrieve my phone, still laughing. Looking at the screen, her smile dropped. "It's your mom."

My smile dropped just as hers did and quickly morphed into a frown. "My mom?" I stood and took the phone from her, opening the message.

Sandy

> Hey hon. Looking 4 a place to crash the nxt few weeks. Can I come by?

A soft touch on my arm drew my attention. "Everything okay, Daze?"

Clearing my throat, I locked my phone, ignoring the message. Sliding the phone into my back pocket, I put on a big smile. "Yep, all good." Shifting focus, I scanned Ellie from head to toe. "Damn girl, you look good! Let's get outta here."

As I made my way towards the front door, I realized Ellie hadn't budged an inch. She continued to look after me, wanting more of an explanation. I knew she wanted to know what my mom said and why I didn't respond, but I didn't want to talk about it. I didn't care to talk about it.

Waving my hand, I motioned for her to follow. "Get that sexy ass over here, and let's skedaddle."

Reluctantly, she followed.

The weekends at Wild Cider were always packed, especially when the Assets were playing. Luckily, Brian, the lead singer of the band and Ellie's friend and co-worker, saved us a front table.

Returning to Elle's with two ciders, we sat and watched the band tune and warm up. Behind the drum set, a dark-haired man gently tapped the different drums making up the set. His forearms flexed with each flick of the drumsticks, and I involuntarily bit my lip.

"If I knew how hot the drummer was, I would've watched the Assets play a long time ago." I stared over the lid of my glass as I sipped my cider.

"Who? Reid?" Ellie tilted her head. "I never really thought about it. Wait...you've never seen the Assets? Why?"

"Solidarity," I said with a wink. Ellie scoffed, rolling her eyes, knowing what I meant. The band had been trying to get her to sing with them for years, but Ellie's ex never let her go to a show despite how big of a dream it was for Ellie to perform.

Insecure men tend to do mean and controlling shit.

Speeding up his hands and adding his feet, the drummer, Reid I had just learned, began pumping out a little solo. His mouth hung open in concentration and he banged his head with the increasing tempo. His dark hair fell over his forehead, and his tightly trimmed beard added dimension to his face.

Oh yeah, drummers are hot.

"Do you know him? Is he single?"

"I actually don't know...I think so." Ellie scrunched her nose in thought.

My phone vibrated again. Internally, I groaned, knowing already who it was. Looking down, I found another message from my mom.

Sandy

> Don't ignore ur mother.

> I'll b there Wed

Sighing, I contemplated my response. Regret was all I was feeling. Regret that I let her know where I lived. Since I left her behind twelve years ago, I hadn't looked back. I did give her my new number for emergencies, and sent her money now and then.

Misguidedly, I allowed her to stay with me once before. I quickly learned my lesson when she walked in barefoot off the street while I was in the middle of an advanced pottery class. We were in the back room, working on the throwing wheels. To make it to my apartment, she only had to walk straight through the show and painting room; instead, she purposely came into class.

The issue, though, was that she was drunk off her ass, and it was midday. Barely able to walk a straight line, she tripped and fell right on top of a student's clay work in progress. The student was a six-ty-four-year-old retiree who took on pottery as a hobby. While we'd only been working on our vases for thirty minutes, she had been practicing at the wheel for over two years. It was the first time she successfully centered her clay and the look of defeat as my mom crash landed on top of it, broke my heart.

I gave the student a month of free classes, and I gave my mom a swift kick in the ass out the front door the next morning.

Daisy

No, I can't help you this time. Sorry.

Guilt tugged at me as I worried I was being too harsh. The unpleasant feeling was quickly washed over with pride at drawing a boundary. This was why I moved away after all. My mother may have controlled my first eighteen years of life, but I was in control now.

In silence, Ellie and I watched as the band introduced themselves. The man with a guitar played the opening chords to "Paint it, Black" by The Rolling Stones, and Reid came in hot with the drums. *Holy shit.* I was in love...at least for tonight.

two

reid

NUMBERS, NUMBERS. INVOICES, INVOICES. My day passed quickly as I reconciled the remaining balances on our larger accounts. When you learn how to add two plus two before the age of three, that means you're destined to be an accountant. Or at least work with money in some way.

Or so my parents decided. I was sure it didn't help that my family lineage was made up of accountants. I was fully aware of how silly that may have sounded to someone outside of the family, but in our family, it was serious.

My father. My father's father. My father's father's father. And so it went. All made their way up the chain, eventually landing in a CFO or VP of Finances position. Throw in a little bit of stock trading and you have a recipe for old family money, nepotism, and high expectations.

The way it was pressured on me as a kid, you would think that our family was a long line of war heroes. Thirty years and a master's degree later, I was a Senior Accountant at the local marketing agency. As much as I lacked passion for accounting, I enjoyed it enough. Numbers didn't lie or manipulate; I held the power. *Insert evil laugh.*

A hand slapped the doorjamb at the entrance of my shared office.

"Yo, I'm headed out." Looking up, Brian, my friend, bandmate, and fellow accountant, leaned in. "See you at six thirty?"

"You know it," keeping my eyes glued to the screen, I snapped my fingers and shot a finger gun at him over my monitor. I listened as his laughter retreated down the wall.

Shutting down my computer, putting my calculator back in its assigned spot in the top left drawer, and rolling my chair back into place, I headed out the door. My phone rang as I walked through the parking lot. With a sigh, I clicked the button to answer.

"Hey mom."

"Reid, sweetie, I'm calling to see what time you'll be by this evening." My mom's voice carried through the speakers as the Bluetooth in my car automatically connected. Per usual, she skipped the pleasantries and went right into her agenda.

"Hi mom, I'm good. How are you?" Annoyingly, I tried to force the conversation.

Her light laughter filled the car. "Reid, such a jokester. Yes, hello darling. I'm well. I was just confirming when you'll be by later."

"Well, seeing as how we haven't talked about it, I wasn't planning on coming by. I have plans." My parents were blissfully unaware of my drumming hobby, and I planned to keep it that way.

The only acceptable musical hobby to my parents was piano or violin, both of which I learned as a child. Both of which I still play, but nothing compares to the drums. The beat that thrums through my body, the way my whole body works, and the power the music holds.

"We're having the Dickover's for dinner, and I expect you to be there," my mother's words came out exasperated, as if I should have already known the evening's plans. "They're bringing Elizabeth."

The mention of Liz's name sent my eyes rolling so hard it had hurt. Biting the inside of my cheek, I tried to hide my annoyance over the phone line. For years my parents had been priming a marriage between Liz and me, despite how much I've protested. Now that I was thirty, the pressure had increased, and we were teetering on the verge of an arranged marriage.

"Sorry to disappoint, mom, but I won't be there. As I said, I have plans."

"That just won't do, Reid. What is so important?" The tone of her voice was a silent challenge. If my mother had a special skill, it was manipulation. My therapist might say this is why I take to accounting so well. My therapist might then say it's because it allows me to control something in my life.

"I made plans with my friends, and it would be rude to cancel. Had you told me earlier about the dinner, I would have planned to be there instead. Sorry mom, tell the Dickover's I said 'hi.'"

With my eyes fixed on the road, I zoned out as mom's voice faded into the background, her words about prioritizing family blending into the silence.

Stopping home, I took a quick shower before changing into an outfit more supportive of performing rock music than my button-up ironed shirt and slacks. Time was tight as I ran right back out the door. I had the foresight to pack my drums in their cases the night before, after practice, but I still had to stop by Brian's to load them in the car. Regardless of how popular we were locally, we were still an after-work garage band, which meant we didn't have a caddy.

Rushing past my roommate, Chuckie, I gave a small salute. Chuckie, his mouth full of cereal, gave me a silent nod as I locked the door behind me. I made a decent enough living that I didn't need a roommate, but a roommate was a convenient excuse to not have a guest room or entertain my parents too often.

My parents were wonderful parents. I loved them as an only child did, but I enjoyed being able to keep my life separate from them. They had held enough influence over me my whole life; I figured the more

I established myself away from them, the more seriously they'd take me. Yet, the fact that they still continued to refuse to acknowledge my denial of a marriage, or even relationship, with Liz, though, proved to me otherwise.

Our gig was at the local brewery, Wild Cider. The place was guaranteed to be slammed on a weekend, and even more so when we played. Over the last few years, we'd gained a bit of local notoriety. Everyone loved classic rock, and those that didn't could at least appreciate our punny name. Brian, Kara, Louis and I not only rocked out together, but we also worked together as accountants; thus, The Assets were born.

With Kara on bass, Louis on lead guitar, Brian as the lead singer and back-up guitarist, and me on drums, we could crank out just about any song that made you involuntarily head bang.

Brian excelled in his role as lead singer, but for the last few years, we'd been trying to get our co-worker, Ellie, to join him and share the spotlight. The woman had pipes. But every time we'd finally convinced her to come out, her ex wouldn't let her get past the front door.

So, today, when she finally made an appearance, it was no surprise to me when Brian called her onstage to sing with us. It was evident by the way her mouth hung open, her jaw dragging on the ground, that she had no idea of his plan.

When not on stage, Ellie danced with a petite blonde woman. Her long and wavy hair dipped past her waist, grazing her ass every time she swayed. Playful pink strands littered her golden locks, and when the overhead string lights hit her just right, she'd glisten. She was star plucked from the night sky that hung above.

Her flowy dress floated above the ground as she glided between the drunk dancers. The skirt was covered in patterns of different colors and shapes; it made absolutely no sense, yet also made absolutely total sense.

Waving her arms and bouncing on her toes, she swirled around Ellie, who was lost in the music herself.

The way this woman was so free, I found myself wondering if I was imagining it. How did she move as if nothing tethered her to reality? As if it was her world, and we all just existed to fill the space in between her movements. In my world of structure and conformity, she was a welcomed bright streak.

Closing out with Journey's classic, "Don't Stop Believin'," the night was a smash. As the night's entertainment switched over to the speakers playing pop music controlled by the bartenders, people milled about, sipping their dwindling drinks while we cleaned up. This was usually the part of the night where a few courageous spectators would chance coming up to try hitting on one of us.

A busty woman wearing a ripped shirt, showing her cleavage down to her naval, moved to stand in front of me. Placing her hands in her back pockets, she approached casually, but the man in me couldn't miss how the stance made her chest a little more pronounced. The overt peacocking never did much for me, but she was pretty, and I wasn't one to be rude.

She spoke first, with a small "hey." My quick nod was a brief acknowledgement as I packed up my drums. "You're really good at the drums."

"Thanks," I offered a small smile before moving to place the cymbals in their round bags.

She toed at the ground, not making a move to leave. "So...what's your name?"

"Reid."

"Oh, okay Doctor Reid." I raised an eyebrow at her in question. "Oh, my God!" she called in shock. "You don't know who Doctor Reid is? Spencer Reid? *Criminal Minds?* It's only, like, the best murder show there is. And Reid is a total hottie. Everyone has a crush on him. There was this one episode where he was being questioned by a panel and this Senator man was all, 'be calm agent,'" she mimicked a deep baritone voice. "And Reid was all like 'This is calm, and it's Doctor.'"

She got lost in rehashing other storylines of this crime show thing. I do my best to feign interest, but I couldn't stop my attention from drifting behind her. Ellie and her mystery friend laughed with Brian, and her gold hair glistened, calling me like the North star.

"So, what're you up to after this?" My attention was pulled back as the scantily clothed woman tugged at my shirt.

Gently removing her hand from me, I took a step back. Being touched, unprompted, was one of my personal hells. "Not to be rude, but I'm not interested."

"Wow, just like that, huh?" she seemed to puff her chest out a little more.

"Yep, not really looking for anything right now." Zipping my last travel case, I offered her a small, friendly smile. "Kara's on the market, though, if you're interested."

I had caught my bass playing bandmate checking out the woman in front of me a few times throughout the night. And despite Kara chatting with a group of people, and the woman making conversation with me, Kara kept her gaze on us. On cue, she turned to look at Kara and they made eye contact. I chuckled to myself as I watched them give each other a knowing look.

"Huh, thanks." The ripped shirt woman sauntered over to Kara, who in one swoop put her arm around her and ushered her into a dark corner. It felt like I'd just done a good deed.

Smirking to myself, I loaded up the bags. With one strapped to my front, one hanging off my back, and a stacked roller cart, I made my way to my car.

"Bye Reid!" a voice called. Looking over, I found Ellie waving from her spot by Brian, who lifted his hand in acknowledgement. The blonde and pink haired pixie gave a small wave as well. Intrigued and in a trance, I waved back.

three

reid

"HI MOM," GROGGILY, I wiped the sleep from my eyes and glanced at the clock next to my bed. Nine a.m. on a Saturday. *Why?*

"Reid, darling, I hope I didn't wake you. Anyhow, it's nine a.m., you should have started your day by now." She never missed an opportunity to "gently guide" me, as she so put it. "I'm calling to invite you to brunch tomorrow morning. Hopefully, *this* is enough notice."

Groaning, I wasn't ignorant of her subtle jab based on yesterday's call. Anyone would agree that twenty-four-hour notice was the bare minimum. "Sure, mom. I'll be there."

"Fantastic. Be here at half-past nine, sharp."

"Nine thirty? Mom, brunch literally means breakfast-lunch. Meaning normal people don't start it until eleven. Ten thirty at the earliest."

"Well, we are not normal people, are we, dear?"

"That's for sure," I snorted sarcastically, trying to keep my volume low.

"I am going to ignore that little quip. We will see you tomorrow, dear. Love you."

"Yep, love you." Standing, I tossed my phone on the bed and opened my curtains. The early morning sun brightened the room.

Reaching my arms above my head, I yawned whilst stretching the laziness out of my muscles.

What was I to do on a Saturday morning at nine? Typically, I was still in dreamland, having just won a Grammy or an epic battle with a super villain who shot green goo from his eyes. Sitting back on my bed, I picked up my electric drumsticks and began freestyling on my air drums.

My phone vibrated with a notification and a text from my bass player filtered through.

Kara

Thanks for playing wing man last night. I owe you one.

Reid

Ha, my pleasure

Kara

Ok, Chick-fil-a employee

I got you next time.

Reid

Not needed.

Kara

Come on, mister dark and broody. You don't want to be alone forever

Reid

I have you ;)

Ending my message with a kissy face emoji, I locked my phone and went to start my day. *Mother would be so proud.*

It wasn't that I wanted to be alone forever, and it wasn't that I was dark and broody. I just didn't see the appeal in giving someone so much power. For now, I was happy with my drums and my numbers.

Approaching the large two-story ornate home, I straightened my jacket, brushed back my hair, and fixed the bouquet of flowers so the snapdragons were at the perfect height.

"Darling," my mom answered the door with flair, "are those for me?"

Despite bringing her flowers from her favorite farmer vendor every time I visited, she always acted with the same surprise. "Oh, these are positively lovely." Taking the bouquet from me, she buried her face in the petals, breathing in deeply. "You look handsome as ever," she observed, giving me a once over after lightly embracing me.

"Thanks mom."

I led myself through the front foyer into the formal dining room where my dad was already seated reading the morning newspaper. His right leg was casually crossed over his left, and he was already dressed in pressed slacks and a neatly buttoned-up shirt—his version of dressing down.

"Good morning, son." Letting the lip of the paper dip, dad surveyed me. "Looking good. Dina is just finishing up the crepes. Come have a seat." Referencing their personal chef, he folded his paper and gave me his attention. "So, tell me. How's life?"

"Don't start without me!" mom called from the kitchen, where I'm sure she was arranging the flowers in a vase.

Rolling his eyes, dad leaned back in this chair and crossed his arms. "You'd think we were about to discuss world secrets."

"Speaking of which, the President should be calling any minute. We need to discuss bullet points before the briefing with NATO," I joked in a flat tone.

"Ha, ha. Always so funny, Reid." Mom fluttered through the swinging door that led from the kitchen to the dining room. Patting my shoulder on the way to her seat, she kissed my dad's cheek in the process.

Dina followed closely with a stack of crepes. "Hey Dina," I greeted, hungrily eyeing the world's best crepes. "How's Toby?" I asked.

Her son, Toby, was starting in martial arts at the same dojo I started at when I was six. With my heart still tied to the sport and the dojo, I was particularly interested in his progress.

Her face lit up at the mention of her son. "Excited. He can't wait to challenge you to a sparring match," she said with an enormous smile.

Grabbing one of the thin pancakes, I piled on cream cheese filling and fresh strawberries. "Name the time and place, and I'll be there. But make sure he knows I'm not going to let him win just because his mom is my favorite cook."

With a giggle and nod, she disappeared as quickly as she had entered. Looking up, I found both my parents eyeing me expectantly. "Is everything alright?"

"Of course," mom laughed and fidgeted with her napkin. "Are you free this Friday, Reid?"

"Yes..."

"Lovely. We scheduled you a date with Liz at that quant pottery shop in town."

"Mom," I rubbed my forehead in frustration. "I already told you I am not interested in a relationship with Liz. I really wish you would stop pushing the issue."

"Son," dad interjected. "Your mother just wants what is best for you. You haven't brought home a girl since college, and you're thirty. It is the natural progression of life to move on to the next step. A wife. A baby. A house."

Choking on a strawberry, I chugged a glass of orange juice. "A baby and a house? What the hell are you talking about?"

"Language." Mom gasped, her mouth agape. "One date with Liz, Reid. She's a lovely girl and her parents are dear friends. We've already made reservations and confirmed with Liz, anyhow. It would be rude to cancel."

"It sure would, so best you make that call today so as to not upset her any further."

"Reid Malcom Flores," my dad's voice grew stern. "Be the gentleman I raised you to be and attend the date with Liz."

My jaw ticked, and I felt transported to childhood. The day I told my family I wanted to take the STEM course in high school, to eventually major in robotics in college, had been engrained in my brain. Instead of hearing me out, they bore into me the family line of business and financial executives.

You will take the business course. Be the person I raised you to be.

The finality of my dad's words made me rebel. I gave my parents a fake course consent form for business, then photoshopped my dad's signature onto the course consent form for STEM. Dad was on the phone with my Aunt Suzy the minute he saw my class schedule through the student portal. Within a week, I was living with my aunt a state away. Apparently, the lesson was to learn to appreciate the life my parents were trying to get me to build for myself.

Placing my fork down, I patted at the corners of my mouth. Jumping out the window seemed a potential avenue of escaping, yet also drastic considering the door was right there. Running to a hidden midwestern town and becoming a recluse seemed like a pipedream. Sighing, I stood, pushing my chair away.

"I will go on the date with Liz, but this is the one and only time. Do not make plans for me again like this, or that will be the end of our relationship. You do not get to control who I see, or what I do."

"That's not what we're trying to do," mom's eyes flooded with tears. Her voice shook as she sniffled. "I just want to see you happy."

"I *am* happy. That's what you don't seem to understand. This, *this*," I said, using my index finger to draw a big circle around the three of us, "makes me unhappy; but I will do this once. Just once. For you."

Unsure of how many ways I could make it any clearer, I left it at that and turned on my heels.

four

daisy

"Ring-a-ding!" a chipper, balding, older aged man in a postal uniform called as he entered through the front door.

"Marty! How the hell are ya'?" I cheerfully returned the greeting, excited to see Marty's happy, familiar face. The town's mailman was an everyday highlight. I loved hearing stories about his grandkids, and the tub of extra cookies his wife made he brought every Monday.

He held out a stack of envelopes and paper ads. "Same as every day. I woke up to another beautiful day. Soph hit a homer yesterday, so we treated her to a sundae."

"Go Soph!" I flipped through the stack and landed on the shining ad. Dropping all the other papers, I brought the glossy paper closer to my face to read.

"What you got there?"

"A flyer for The National Pottery and Ceramics Showcase." My eyes glazed over as I soaked in the newsletter. A gorgeous blue and orange pot sat on the cover. Delicate scenery had been carved into the clay, painting a picture of a meadow and deer running through. "Macy Shivers. I'd know her work anywhere. My clay idol."

Marty chortled across from me. "You in the exhibit this year?"

"I wish!"

"Well, heck Daisy. You're as good as any." Shaking my head in disagreement, Marty laid a thick hand on my shoulder. "One day maybe you'll be some other little girl's clay idol."

Laughing together, we missed the chime of the door opening. In unison, we both jumped when a raspy voice unexpectedly spoke up from behind his round figure. "What's so funny?"

I knew that voice. Years of chain smoking and chugging beers weighed on the once delicate tone. Raspiness took over; a raspiness that conveyed tiredness and hopelessness.

"Just an inside joke." Marty inclined his head toward the petite intruder with a polite smile. "I best get goin'. The missus is making her famous meatloaf for dinner." Throwing a small wave over his shoulder, he left me and my mother alone.

"Mom. What're you doing here?"

"Come on' Daze. Is that any way to greet your mom?" Opening her arms, she motioned for me to step in.

I sighed, not particularly keen on this exchange. Ignoring her invitation for affection, I crossed my arms confidently. Come on Daze, stand your ground.

"I thought I told you not to come by."

"Daisy, please. Don't make your mom beg." She dropped her arms dramatically and began fidgeting. "Listen, Carl hasn't been treatin' me right and I'm finally leavin'. I'm finally makin' my own way. Like my strong daughter."

"You're still with that guy?"

"Well, not no more. Didn't you hear me? I'm finally leavin' him." She huffed in exasperation and her small smile dropped. My heart tugged at her defeat.

"You were 'finally leaving him' three years ago. Then the year before that. Then don't forget about the accide-"

"I'll never forget that." She cut me off sternly, anger coating her features. "I know I ain't got the best record of leavin', but I am this time. Really."

The self-soothing of her rubbing her own arm caught my attention. Her eyes were downcast, and she avoided looking directly at me now. A light green mark was fading along her left bicep, and I finally noticed a similar mark under her right eye.

"Alright, let me see your eye." I took her face in my hands and paused, taking in her sunken cheeks, chapped lips, and frizzy hair. "Okay, but remember the rule?"

"You're my child, Daisy. Remember?" Rather than answer with venom, I stayed quiet. I was her child, and I'd been let down one too many times. Too many times I was forced into being the grown-up. Reading the silent message behind my eyes, she curved her shoulders inward in a slump. "Yes, I remember."

Two days passed without incident. Nary a beer bottle or mini shooter in sight.

My coffee maker sputtered to a stop. Clutching the wonky shaped "mug" one of my students made on their first pottery throwing attempt, I sipped the velvety caramel colored goodness. Taking in the crumpled quilt on the couch, I was unsure where mom had gone for the morning. She'd at least kept to her promise of no alcohol while staying here. That I knew of.

A glossy paper caught my eye, drawing me back to the ad for the National Pottery and Ceramics Showcase for the zillionth time. The showcase was something I had always dreamed of attending, especially as a featured artist, but I knew deep down it was just a fantasy. Every full moon I would pull my crystals together, write my little manifestation of attending the showcase, then burn it in the flame of whatever candle I could find. Manifesting would only get me so far, though, and I was me, after all. Many took in my image of carefreeness and recklessness, assuming I moved with the wind. That was somewhat true, but since getting my feet on the ground, I've liked it that way.

Routine had become a comfort .

Bills to pay? That meant I had a roof over my head. Nice.

Alarm waking me up in the early morning? That meant I had clients to serve. Even better.

When I had rent to pay and my own financial security to ensure, throwing around money wasn't a luxury I particularly cared for.

Chewing my bottom lip, I took in the pot again. This time, I noticed little rodents combing through the grass. Macy Shivers was a goddamn genius.

"Fuck it," I said to no one but myself. My fingers flew across my screen, and several clicks later I had my ticket and hotel room secured. I was finally going to the National Pottery and Ceramics Showcase, bitches.

A banner flashed across my phone screen. I groaned at the message I just knew was coming.

Calley

> Hi Daisy, I'm so sorry. I have a tennis match tonight and won't be able to make it in for my shift.

Daisy

> I asked you to get me your schedule so we could plan for this. It's really irresponsible to continue to call out like this.

I loathed having to play the stern boss role.

Calley

I'll pick up an extra shift next week to help.

Daisy

That doesn't help me tonight. We have a full paint and sip night.

Calley

I'm so sorry. I'll call Liam to see if he can help. Coach says if I miss this match, I'm out for the next three matches.

Dang it. I had a soft spot for her, and she knew it; Calley, while irresponsible with her planning, was whip smart and a crazy good tennis player. She'd been working for me since she was fifteen, and in the last two years I've attended a few matches myself. Watching her grow as a young woman and a soon-to-be pro-athlete, I had become invested in her success in a way.

Daisy

We can't have your generation's Venus Williams missing a match.

Alight, but I'm serious. Get me your schedule by Monday.

Calley

I promise!! Liam said he'll be there!

Okay. At least that meant I had Liam. Another text quickly came in, this time from my savior of an employee.

Liam

Calley just called. I'll be in at four to begin set-up.

Daisy

The man of the hour! Yes! Thank you, Liam!

His only reply was a thumbs-up emoji. Brief, but I'd take it. *Youths.* I made a mental note to reach out to the local rehabilitation center with a job posting. Slay & Clay had been booming, and I'd been meaning to bring in additional employees. A pickle like this was a wake-up call.

Kip, my last hire from the center, took to clay so well he went on to win a scholarship to the Pennsylvania Academy of the Fine Arts. Nine hundred and thirty-four days sober, and a year into his degree in Sculpture, he was making a new way for himself. He always had it in him. I just provided him with an opportunity.

That was something I always promised myself I would do the day I opened my own studio. Sometimes I wondered if mom was given a chance to pursue her passions, she'd stay sober too. Instead, we jumped from town to town, following man to man, and staying in motel after motel. The drabness of waitressing in back-of-the-woods shacks and bars weighed on mom, making it hard for her to ignore the call of the drink.

At least that was her reasoning every time I begged her to try for a new life. For us.

five

daisy

MOM STILL HADN'T RETURNED by four, but there was nothing I could really do about it. She was a grown woman. She could come and go as she pleased, as long as she stayed true to her promise. As the minutes ticked by though, I grew less and less confident in her coming through the front door right as rain.

The ringing of the studio phone pulled me from my thoughts. It wasn't uncommon for people to call prior to a paint and sip class asking about drink selection or rules about outside food.

Leaning over the wooden counter, I picked up the receiver. "Slay and Clay," I said in my cheery, customer service voice.

"Yeah, put Sandy on," a gruff voice filtered through.

Unease crept into my chest. Who was calling for my mom and how did they know she was here? "Sorry, I think you have the wrong number."

"You the girl?" Silence hung between us. "Daisy? Remember me?" Bile turned in my gut as I realized I knew that voice. It was the one I heard in my nightmares. The same voice that gave me night sweats and kept me from ever returning to Maryland.

Carl.

"Of course I remember you, you rat bastard. Though, to be honest, I'm both surprised and disappointed to learn you've lived this long. Putting my life at risk wasn't enough, you had to-"

"-still a little bitch, I see. Just like your mother. Put that whore on the phone."

"Gonna be honest, Carl, there's a tree out there somewhere working really hard to replace the oxygen you're wasting. I'm gonna save it some work and end this conversation here." I slammed the receiver down, cutting off his rage filled voice before he had a chance to respond.

Thank goodness Liam agreed to cover for Calley. A full house meant there would be thirty people crammed in my front studio space looking to get warm on wine while letting their creative juices flow. Liam prepped the side bar area, while I made sure each seat had glazes and tools within reach.

Ten minutes before class was scheduled to start, the first group arrived. Four cozy friends showed up, decked out in sweatpants and baggy shirts—my kind of gals. They took their seats, giggling with their glasses of wine. The minutes passed as more clients walked in, each settling in a seat as I directed them to get comfortable.

Angels broke out in a drum solo and a spotlight shined on the door as a familiar face walked in. I would know, given I'd fantasized of him every night since the last show at Wild Cider. The tall, slim but built, clean cut, handsome man with muscular forearms held the door open for a petite brunette.

His slim, dark washed jeans fitted his muscular thighs perfectly, and his henley stretched against his tight chest. The rolled-up sleeves were the icing on the cake. Framing his eyes were wire-rimmed glasses he didn't wear on stage, but as I looked at him, they fit him perfectly. In contrast, the woman was dressed like she was ready for brunch or teatime. White and pink wove in a plaid pattern on the jacket and skirt of her tweed two-piece set.

"Welcome to Slay & Clay," I said, offering my friendly business owner smile. "You can place your bag up there. Underneath, you'll also find aprons to wear. You'll want one so you don't risk ruining your clothes."

In an attempt to not gawk at the handsome musician, I turned to find someone else to talk to. Waving at a regular, who used the weekly paint and sip class as herself-care from her three kids and husband, I allowed myself to be pulled into riveting conversation about soccer game and science fair updates. A moment later, alight tap on my shoulder pulled me from my conversation.

"Do you have anything a little more...flattering?" the petite woman from the date with my personal dreamy rockstar asked with a look of disgust on her face. We both looked down at the apron that barely hung from around her neck, untied around her waist.

"Nope," I popped the "p" and gave a light shrug. "You don't have to wear it if you don't want. I just recommend it because the glaze can stain light-colored clothes, like yours."

With a groan, she tied the apron around her waist and returned to my mystery drum man.

The room filled as we waited for a missing a group of three. I decided to wait until five minutes past the scheduled time to start and filled my time helping a couple choose their pottery to paint. A sound caught my attention, followed by a waving hand.

"Waitress," the woman in the tweed waved at me. "Hi, yes, may I have a glass of Chardonnay?"

Walking over, I internally rolled my eyes but did my best to keep a pleasant smile on my face. "Yes, the bar is right over there."

"You're not the waitress?"

"No, there are no servers here. The bar is open, and Liam isn't only a kick-ass artist, but also a killer bartender. You are welcome to get your drinks as you please."

"Oh," she looked at the wooden hutch that we used as a bar with a scowl. "If you're not a waitress, then why are you dressed like that? You must work for tips, no?"

The mystery drummer boy, Reid, I believed Ellie said was his name, turned red. Clearly uncomfortable, he whispered something in his dates ear.

"What? I'm just saying." She responded innocently, loudly enough for me to hear.

Looking down, I took in my outfit. I had chosen overalls in my favorite color, yellow. They had blue embroidered flowers strewn about, and underneath, I wore a white baby tee. My pink converse peaked out from the hem of the pants with a pop of color. My outfit was mostly covered, though, by my large pottery apron. It was one I was proud of, having made it myself. Honestly, I was conservative in picking the fabric for this one, choosing a pale blue.

"This is a pottery apron; it protects my clothes. And I'm not in need of tips. I own this shop. However, our faithful bartender, Liam, happily accepts tips if you're feeling kind enough."

"Hey, miss priss, keep your judgements to yourself," Geraldine, one of my favorite regulars, mater-of-factly called from the table over. "Daisy is an artist, so she wears artists' clothes. Not her fault you know nothing about that."

The small woman gasped and placed a hand over her heart in feigned hurt.

I loved Geraldine. During the day, she worked at the sheriffs office, and in the evenings, she threw some mad clay. My favorite of hers was a compartmentalized charcuterie board. For one. I used that sucker almost daily.

While I was thankful for her defense, a tanking on my online reviews was not something I wanted. And the pampered woman in a matching tweed suit gave off *"I leave bad reviews for any minor inconvenience"* vibes.

Diffusing the situation, I clapped my hands. "Alright ladies, less gabbing, more dabbing! Let's get started, shall we?"

Turning on my heels to address the room, I gave Geraldine a discreet wink.

Throughout the event the tweed clad woman carried on, clearly unhappy. Between attempting flirty touches with Reid, she would send me sneers. Fine by me. I'd had worse thrown at me. I could handle a cranky, privileged, entitled girly pop.

"Alright friends, it's been a lovely evening!" I clap as I address the room. "Please begin wrapping up your creations and place them on the table up front, with your tag under it. If you forget to tag it, I won't know it's yours! I'll text you in five to seven days once it's been fired and is ready for pickup."

Various shouts of *thank you* came from around the room of people as they shuffled, placing their painted creations on the designated table. The sound of glass breaking pulled my attention back to the table with Reid and his date.

"Oops," the woman shrugged, the sound of her shoes crunching as she walked over broken glass and spilled wine.

"Liz, seriously?" Reid groaned. "We need to clean this up. Can you get me some paper towels? I need to make sure no one else steps on the glass."

"Why? Isn't that her job?" She nodded in my direction with a shit-eating grin.

"Again, I'm not a server, nor a janitor, but yes. I will take care of it."
Working to grab the roll of paper towels we keep on hand behind the
bar for the inevitable spills, I waved Reid off. "Please, no worries. I got
it."

He stood and ushered his date, Liz, out the door, his face coated
in unhappiness. I watched as he waved his hands on the sidewalk,
speaking angrily at the woman. A vein popped in his neck, and I wasn't
going to lie...it was kind of hot. As he waved his hands around, the
hem of his shirt lifted a little and I caught a glimpse of the coveted V
dipping below the waist of his jeans.

"Wow, she sucked," Liam blew out, stepping around me to pick up
the discarded paintbrushes. I only chuckled in response, focused on
picking up the larger pieces of glass.

A ding signaled the opening of the front door. I looked up to find
the stud drummer approaching, a frown on his face. "I apologize. That
was really rude." He squatted down to my level and started helping me
carefully pick up every piece we could with our hands. "Please, can I
take over?"

Scanning him, I took him in from head to toe. "I promise, it's not
a problem. Go make sure your girlfriend gets home safely. Clearly,
she's a little unsteady." I immediately felt bad for making a quick
judgement. But, then seeing her lean against the shop glass, scrolling
on her phone, not a care in the world, made me not care so much about
being brash.

"She's not my girlfriend," he said a little forcefully. "I called her
a ride, and she's safe. Also, I don't think it was the alcohol. She was
pretty pissed after that lady called her out for being nasty to you."

"She got called out for rude behavior, so she broke a glass? Classy."

"Clearly," he chuckled at my sarcasm, and our eyes locked for a
moment. "Do you have a dustpan?"

"Here you are," Liam approached, holding trusty dusty. "I was going to head out, but I can stay if you need?" He eyed Reid cautiously and I giggled inwardly at his chivalry. As if his twenty-one-year-old slim frame would do anything against the tall, forearm flexing man if he became a threat.

"No need, Liam. Have a good night." I stopped him as he reached the door. "Hey, try to think if you have any referrals for your replacement. We'll need someone lickety-split." With a nod, he was gone. A moment passed before I realized I was left alone with the steamy drummer who I've yet to formally meet.

"You have an interesting vocabulary," he said as he carefully scanned the floor for any stray pieces of glass.

"Do I? Or is everyone else's vocabulary just boring?"

"Well, I guess both could be true." Dumping the last of the glass into the bin, he stood, taking in the full studio space. "So, you own this place?"

"Sure do." I untied my pottery apron, now exposing my outfit in its full glory. Ignoring the heat of his stare, I placed my apron on its designated hook by the front door. "Now, be honest. Does this outfit make me look like I need extra tips? Also, not that it's a bad thing. I feel like she made it seem like a bad thing."

"Liz grew up without any knowledge of a world beyond the one she was raised in, which was..." he searched for the right word. But I knew what he was getting at.

"Privileged?"

He winced at that, seemingly uncomfortable with calling his date that, though it seemed most accurate. "I suppose. But anyway. No, I like your outfit. It's spunky. You do look the part of an artist."

"Well, dandy. That's what I was going for."

"Dandy?" He chuckled at the word and looked around the room again. "Did you make all these?"

"Most of them. This wall here highlights pieces from students of past classes. Once they reach the Great Creator stage, they have the option of using my store to sell their pieces. Then they can choose to put their profit back into their studio account or request a pay-out. Most use it to pay for additional art supplies. Or they sell their pieces as an independent artist on their own."

I scanned the wall of varying sculptures and vases. Pointing to the front half of the wall, and the varying pillars, I singled out my personal makes. "These are mine."

Silently, he walked around, assessing each piece, sometimes nodding, sometimes humming.

"Not gonna lie. You're making me a little nervous." I chuckled.

Locking eyes with me, he gave me a bright smile. "I was just appreciating your work. Can I ask why pottery?"

"I suppose with any art, you create what you want. There are no rules. In pottery specifically, the clay is malleable. I can make one thing, change my mind, then make it something else entirely. I control the outcome. In painting, if you make a mistake, you can try to cover it up, or make it fit. In sewing, you can rip seams, but you'll still have the holes where the needle punched. In pottery, you can smash it down and try again.

"I get to turn a wet lump into a vase. Or sculpture. Or cup. Then someone buys that vase and I become a piece of their home."

Humming appreciatively, he nodded. "I get it. That's what I like about numbers."

"Numbers? Someone buys your numbers and they become a piece of their home?"

"No," he chuckled, rubbing at his stubbled jaw. "The control piece. I'm an accountant. Numbers don't lie, they can't change. Addition is addition, subtraction is subtraction."

"An accountant? I thought you were a drummer?" Both our heads cocked to the side in curiosity, like two puppies meeting each other for the first time and deciding if they want to play. "I saw you play at Wild Cider the other week," I explained.

"I thought you looked familiar. You're friends with Ellie, right?"

"That's me," blush crept up my cheeks, knowing that he noticed me. "So, an accountant, huh? Numbers by day, drums by night?"

"Got to keep it interesting." He glanced at this watch. "I should get going. It was nice to meet you..."

"Daisy."

"Pretty," he flashed another smile and his eyes crinkled behind his glasses. "I'm Reid."

"Handsome." I retorted, causing his brows to quirk in question. "You said 'pretty' after my name, so I thought I'd return the compliment."

Laughing as he walked out the door, I locked up promptly behind him. Arming the building, I checked all the doors were locked. The quiet was usually a signal to me that the night was over, but with the absence of my mom's chatter, I realized mom still hadn't returned and my stomach churned.

Dialing her number, I patiently listened to the ringing on the other end, hoping that she would pick up. Instead, the automated message greeting played. Sighing, I left a voicemail.

"Hey mom, just checking in. You haven't returned home, and I want to make sure you're okay. I'm locking up. Call me when you get here, and I'll let you in."

The ringing of my phone at full volume pulled me from my fitful sleep. It took me hours to fall asleep, and once I did, I woke up every thirty minutes to check for any missed calls. Sitting up abruptly, a bowl of cereal crashed to the floor. *Dang it.* I really needed to stop falling asleep while eating. At least I had the good sense to not pour milk into the bowl before beginning it to bed.

Quickly grabbing my phone, mom's name scrolled across the screen. Noting the time, I swore. It was nearly two in the morning.

"Hello," I answered, both tired and concerned.

"Day-ze, it's me. Op'n up."

The slur of her words put me on alert. "Mom, have you been drinking?"

"Jus' one. Op'n up." She tried hiding her slur, but instead it was more apparent than before.

Rushing downstairs, I pulled the blinds from the front door to see my mom leaning against the metal frame. Cursing, I disarmed the alarm. A stench of whiskey flooded my senses as I opened the door.

Pushing past me, she stumbled into the front studio area. Keeping one eye on her, I locked back up and re-armed the building. Laced with agitation, I grabbed her elbow and led her up the stairs.

"You promised me you wouldn't drink again while you were here." Anger and disappointment flowed through my veins.

"It wa'z jus' one."

"Clearly not, Sandy." In these moments, I always reverted to calling her by her name. It felt like a cheap shot, but it was habit. Almost a defense mechanism. It helped put distance between us. I had trouble calling her mom when that word had so many memories attached to it.

Mom was for fun days at the beach or mall, binging a medical soap opera together while eating ice cream, and being served soup when I was sick.

Sandy was for these moments, when she was just another person who let me down. When a drink was more important than her daughter. When I was the one caring for her.

"You know the rule. You can stay here tonight, but you need to be gone tomorrow."

"Com'on day'ze... don' be like that, it wa'z jus' one."

Carefully, I helped her lay on the purple velvet couch. In a swoop, I covered her with one of my crochet blankets. Still caring for her, I filled a glass of water and placed it next to her with a bottle of Tylenol. Covered in the afghan, she slipped off to slumber quickly. Looking down at her, the innocence of it all struck me. She looked so fragile, so tired, so helpless.

Before retreating to my bed, I printed off several resources for rehab centers and women's shelters. Quietly, I snuck them in her purse and gave her a kiss on the forehead.

Between soft sobs, I reassured myself that this was the best decision for me and her.

six

reid

MUTING MY PHONE, I declined my mom's inevitable phone call. I was in no mood to hear her badger me about sending Liz home last night. If there was one thing I was keen on, it was respect, and she was straight up disrespectful. Making a rude comment about Daisy's clothes was one thing, but then she had the nerve to purposely break a glass by way of a tantrum.

She was pretty pissed when I told her I was calling her an Uber so I could stay behind to help clean up. But to be honest, I didn't care. Even so, I was a gentleman, and made sure she got home safe.

The blonde firecracker had been on my mind since. I couldn't shake the power of her presence, and when she commented on my drumming, it triggered the recent memory of the golden-haired woman at our last show. Even then, though, she held more familiarity that I couldn't pinpoint.

Unable to sleep, I tossed and turned most of the night. Her blue eyes filled my vision every time I tried closing my eyes. It was early, early enough for a morning run before downtown grew too busy. On weekend mornings like this, I liked to take a run through the heart of downtown before the crowds descended.

The town itself was made of quaint buildings of varying designs and vibrant colors. The path from my apartment to town was along a small side road. A farm and its vast land painted one side, a pond on the other. And if I was early enough, Meryl, the owner of the local pastry shop, Meryl's Makes & Cakes, would let me sample her day's selection.

Morning dew sat undisturbed, coating the fields on both sides of me as I paced my way down the winding road. The sun was still rising, and light had just begun touching everything. Geese were out, waddling around like the terrifying creeps they were. Sheep with their baby lambs sat in the farm's grass.

Enjoying the simplicity of the morning, I was in a trance. The speeding police car startled me as it zoomed past from behind. Though silent, the lights were going. I supposed given the earlier hour on a weekend, there was no need for the loud alert, but it sped by, nonetheless.

Reaching downtown, I reveled in the empty streets. The typically packed sidewalks and parking spaces were vacant. Other than the occasional local spending a leisurely morning reading a newspaper on a bench, I was alone to soak it in. That was until the police car from before came into view.

A moment passed before I realized it was parked in front of Slay & Clay. My body reacted involuntarily, the sight making my stomach drop.

Increasing my speed, I ran straight for the shop door that was propped open. From the sidewalk, I observed Daisy in a button up and pants pajama set covered in cartoon bacon and eggs. Her arms were firmly crossed, and her eyes were puffy as she talked to the uniformed police officer.

Knocking lightly on the glass door, I tentatively crossed the threshold.

"Daisy? Is everything alright?"

She turned to me; her red-rimmed eyes wide. "Reid?" Confusion flashed across her face before swiping at a stray tear. "Not quite. I was just telling the officer here that I was robbed."

"Robbed? Are you hurt?" Panic rose, crushing my chest. *Where did that come from?* Keeping my distance, because I hadn't lost all sense, I assessed her.

"Physically, I'm fine. Mentally, I'm...drained. My mother stole three thousand dollars."

"Three thousand? What the hell are you doing leaving that kind of money lying around?" Immediately, I regretted my tone. I hadn't meant to be condescending. Shame filled me as I realized I sounded like my father.

She reared back; her face contorting. I watched as anger took over her features."What the hell are *you* doing coming in here and questioning me while I'm trying to handle this the best I can?"

"Whoa," Kendrick, the officer on the scene, and a local I've known since childhood, stepped in. "Reid, she's right. We're handling the situation the best we can. I would suggest you save your questions for later, *after* Daisy and I have had a chance to finish talking."

"If I even give him the chance," she scoffed under her breath.

"You're right." I held my hands up in surrender. "I'm sorry. It wasn't my place. I just wanted to make sure you're okay."

She put on an overtly fake smile, her lips tight. "Fantastic, thanks."

Retreating, I realized my mistake. My sensibility took over; I just couldn't understand how someone could have that amount of money lying around. And did she say her *mother* stole from her?

I walked the rest of the way to Meryl's shop and ordered two iced lattes to-go and a box of assortments. After letting Meryl know it was a peace offering, she added a few extra mini eclairs and wrapped the paper package with a frilly pink ribbon.

Returning to Slay & Clay, the police cruiser was gone. Kendrick had left, and Daisy sat at the front desk staring angrily at a ledger. Her anger didn't dissipate when she looked up to find me on the other side of the door. Sheepishly, I held up the coffees and box of treats.

Unlocking the door, she propped it open with her foot. "Those better be apology pastries for me, otherwise you're just the jerk who made me feel like shit in a bad situation then came to gloat with sweets not meant for me."

"They are 'I'm very, *very* sorry, let's start over, I promise I'm not a dick' sweets, and... an iced latte."

Pursing her lips, she eyed me for a minute. Her narrowed eyes returned to normal, and she opened the door to me. "Alright. Apology accepted."

Opening the box, she groaned and picked up a mini eclair. Doing my best to not focus on her very distracting moans, I observed the ledger on the counter.

"Do you mind?"

"As long as I get all the eclairs, you can do whatever you want."

Quirking an eyebrow, I kept my interpretation of *whatever I want* to mean only the ledger.

Taking a big bite out of her pastry, she launched in an explanation with a full mouth. "I'm working out balances while I wait for the insurance pay-out. The cash taken was a deposit meant for drop-off today. It's the cash received from sales of items from the last month." She paused, wiping cream from the side of her mouth. "I don't typically keep such a high volume of cash on hand. It was just a busy month with a few craft fairs and showcases.

"I promised my clients their payouts would be available by the end of the day Monday, and the insurance claim won't come through for another two weeks, so I need to figure this out. I hate to have to pull from my savings."

Nodding, I took in her story and guilt racked me again, thinking about my hasty judgment earlier. "I see you have a business line of credit, with funds available?"

"Yeah, but that has interest. I'd rather pull from savings and avoid that."

"Well, if the money from insurance comes back in two weeks, you could pay it off before interest accrues."

Biting into another eclair, chocolate smudged the corner of her lip. She was a messy eater and apparently, I found that really endearing.

"That...actually might work."

"Then you can save your savings in case another emergency comes up."

She snorted at that. "You mean if my mother comes back?"

Unsure of what to say, I stuttered. Instead, I wiped at the corner of her mouth. "Chocolate." With a lopsided grin, I licked the chocolate off my finger without thinking.

Her eyes grew to the size of saucers, and I feigned a cough to ease the tension. The shrill ring of my phone broke our simmering eye contact. *Mom* flashed across the screen, and I quickly muted the call *again*.

"I should, uh, get going. Enjoy the pastries." As I stood, she mimicked the movement. Nodding at me, she rocked on her heels, sipping from her latte. "If you're around tomorrow morning, I can bring you a new batch of sweets to try?"

"Why not? That bad boy is adjustable," she pointed to the clay apron hanging next to the door. "I'm looking forward to it."

seven

daisy

"Ho, HEY, HO, HEY, ho, hey, ho," I sang to myself along with Naughty By Nature to "Hip Hop Hooray" as I worked bits of flattened clay. Rapping with the fast-paced lyrics, I joined the pieces of clay together, gently shaping their curves and ends with a wet brush.

Thankful for Reid's idea yesterday with the line of credit, I felt a bit of a weightlift off my shoulders. The stress of Sandy still weighed on me, but having not heard from her since, there wasn't much I could do, anyway. Who knows where she even was at this point? Carl was still calling several times a day, so at least I knew she was staying away from him.

The promise of morning pastries gave me a glimmer of hope. There really was still good in this world. Especially when it was being delivered by a hunky, glasses wearing, numbers crunching drummer.

My morning's mission of preparing twelve plates for their first firing was complete, and I had a little time to myself. A knock at the front door startled me and I jammed the brush into the clay.

Reid awaited me on the other side of the door. Today, he wore faded jeans and a skin tight light gray tee. His muscles were highlighted under the fabric, and I'd be lying if I said it didn't do something to my lady bits.

"As promised," with a smile, he held up a pretty pink box and two freshly poured coffees. It was unfair this type of man existed and I hadn't had a bite of him yet. Smart, musical, ripped *and* thoughtful.

Bowing, I opened the door, inviting him in. "Bless you, holy one."

He paused, his eyes crinkling with laughter. I watched as his eyes scanned me and I remembered that not only was I in my apron, but that I was also wearing pajamas with sleeping sloths on them.

My breath hitched as he reached out to touch me, taking a swipe at my cheek. Memory of him wiping chocolate from my mouth yesterday, then licking it, replayed in my head. I did my best to hide my gulp.

Pulling his hand away, he assessed it. "Working on something?" Only then did I notice the clay on his finger he must've pulled away from my face.

"Care to see?"

Leading him into the back studio, I proudly stopped in front of my work in progress. Bits of clay laid on the station. Chaotic to the unassuming eye, it was very methodical to me.

"It will be called *Dark Parts Bloom*. Right now, I'm working on the flower pieces that will erupt from a caved chest."

He lightly grazed the freshly pierced piece. "What is this meant to be?"

"A petal," I chuckled, "your knock scared me, and I accidentally pressed too hard."

"Oh man, I'm sorry."

"Don't be." I took the clay and pinched the hole closed before reworking the shape. "That's what I love about clay. Nothing is permanent that you don't want to be. The creator controls the outcome."

Laying the newly formed petal on the workbench, I washed my hands and removed my apron. Signaling him to follow, we reentered the front room and sat across from each other at a table.

Sipping coffee and sampling crumpets and scones, the street outside the front windows remained mostly undisturbed. The quiet Sunday morning was peaceful in the small town, and the company was welcomed.

"So, how do you know Ellie?" Reid picked at an orange cranberry scone.

"We both worked at Loop & Scoop, up the road. The owner's son was a total perv. I put him in his place when he tried to get handsy with her and we've been besties ever since."

"I respect that...one time, we were playing a show, and I threw one of my drum sticks at some guy who slapped a waitresses' ass."

Choking on my coffee, my eyes nearly bugged out of my head. "You didn't!"

"Sure did. Respect is a big value of mine, and he was already causing problems. He was shouting a bunch, and I could tell people around him were uncomfortable. When he smacked her as she walked away, I just," he mimed flicking a drumstick, "without thinking. The only problem was that we were being scouted that night to open for a major country singer. Needless to say, we didn't get it. The band was pretty pissed at me after."

"No way! Who?" I asked, unable to hide my surprise. I knew the Assets were good, but I didn't know they were open-for-a-famous-singer good. Also, did they let cover bands do that?

"Taylor Black?"

"What is it with that guy? I hear his name everywhere." I rolled my eyes at the mention of Ellie's favorite artist, whom she takes every free moment to push on me.

"He's a pretty great lyricist. You don't like him?"

"I don't care for him, but Ellie loves him. She had a weekend in the city planned with her ex and wants to turn it into a girl's trip to see him play a coffee house."

"Her ex? I didn't know they broke up."

"Yep," I said with a pop. "And thank goodness for that. He was a total dick. Never let her leave the house, always telling her what to do. She's finally living for herself again."

"Huh...I was wondering what prompted her to come out and sing with us. We'd been trying to get her to sing with us for years."

"You can thank Shane-can't-keep-it-in-his-pants for that." He whistled at the realization of the name I made for Ellie's cheating ex. "Speaking of your music, tell me more. Why do you do it? What do you like about it? Why the drums? And why are drummers so sexy? Is there criteria you have to meet before you get to pick up the sticks?"

My second to last question made him break into a panty dropping grin.

"Well...I do it because I like it. I like it just because I do. The drums are fun, total babe magnet." He winked at me. "You think I'm sexy? And there were no criteria I had to meet that I know of, but tell me more about the sexy thing."

"Nice try, fisherman. Cast your line somewhere else to fish for more compliments."

A dimple flashed with his chuckle, and he ruffled his hair. "In honesty, the drums are powerful, complex, and well controlled. Think of the feeling you get in your chest when a heavy kick drum starts. Think of the way your head involuntarily moves when the drums join in. There's that and there's the fact that while there is a science to playing them, it's also all feeling. It is freeing in the most calculated sense."

Silence hung as I processed his response. I understood, and it seemed he could tell I did. We stared at each other, unmoving. The jarring ringing of the front phone pulled us from our trance. Once again, we had fallen into locked gazes, and once again, a phone call interrupted us.

I cursed under my breath as I made my way over to the front desk. "Slay and Clay!"

"Put Sandy on, and don't tell me she ain't there," the heavy, nasty voice filtered through the receiver.

"I don't know if you have really bad critical thinking skills, or are just plain stupid, but for the last time, you scumbag, she isn't here. You have the rest of your life to be a better person. Why don't you start now? Stop. Calling." My voice rose with each word, and I ended the call in a full yell before slamming the phone back onto the receiver.

Reid was at the front desk within a breath, his gray eyes stormy. "Who was that?"

"Just some loser who used to date my mom. He's been calling here every day looking for her, but she left him for good reason. She may have stolen three thousand dollars from me, but at least she isn't anywhere near *him*."

His dark brows knitted together as he tried to make an understanding of what I shared. "That's a lot to process...I'm glad to hear she's away from him, but I'm sorry you're dealing with this. Sounds like he's a real piece of work. Are you in any danger?"

Danger hadn't crossed my mind. But thinking back on our history, I supposed there was potential danger. He ruined the one high school I was finally comfortable at, taking away my only sense of community because of his anger. And, over the years, I'd lost count of the shiners he'd given my mom.

"Nothing I can't handle." I said with a shrug. His eyes softened at that, and the corners of his mouth lifted. Looking into his stormy gray eyes, there was a small flicker of recognition and I think I saw in him that he recognized me, too. *Interesting*.

"I've only known you two days, but I would comfortably bet that there isn't much in the world you couldn't handle."

"That's an...oddly sweet thing to say. Thank you." Looking at the clock, I realized the store was supposed to open in ten minutes, and Calley was due to show up any minute. "Hey, I have to get the day started here, and should probably put on some real clothes. Would you want to grab lunch sometime?"

I ignored the moment of hesitation on his face before he responded with a big smile. "Lunch sounds great."

"Who in the hottie heck was that?" Calley asked, her mouth agape, as we watched Reid walk out the door five minutes later just as she arrived.

"A hottie you would've had the chance to meet if you were here Friday."

"Ouch, boss."

Assuring her I was just joking, I nudged her shoulder and congratulated her on her tennis match victory. The cover of the town newspaper had an in-action pic of her making a serve, and I made a show of framing the picture to hang on the front desk.

Clients started filtering in as the streets awoke to life. Humming a song, I cleaned up my workstation.

eight

reid

"REID MALCOM FLORES, I raised you better than that." I listened patiently as my mom chastised me over the phone. After declining her calls for days, I finally gave in. I would have had to face her scolding eventually for sending my *date* home.

"Apparently, the Dickovers didn't raise Liz better than being rude to...people." I hesitated, getting hung up on what to call Daisy.

"I am sure you are exaggerating. Bob and Elaine are lovely people, and I am sure Elizabeth was raised just as properly."

"Then you'd be wrong," I mumbled.

"Speak up and speak clear, Reid. I cannot hear you when you mumble."

"I will call Liz to apologize."

"You will call Elizabeth to ask her on a second date to apologize in person."

I scoffed at the demand and shook my head. "Uh, no. I won't be doing that."

"Reid-"

"Mom, seriously. Enough." I demanded strongly, seriousness in my tone. "I took Liz on the date you set us up on and it was more than clear we're not compatible. There will not be a second date."

"We'll see about that," she huffed. "Until you can provide a viable and suitable alternative partner, we'll continue to discuss your future with Elizabeth."

Memories of the weekend with Daisy flashed in my mind. My heart fluttered, remembering her laughter, her messy eating, and her passion for her work. *When did that happen?*

"I met someone-"

"You what?" mom's tone sounded panicked. Her breath picked up, and I could hear her pacing. "Reid, can you meet for lunch tomorrow?"

"Sure...what's going on?"

"It's something better discussed in person. Come by the house half past noon tomorrow?"

After all the badgering, I'd thought she'd be happy to hear I was interested in someone. Her quick turn in attitude caught me off guard. I had to meet with her and figure out what the hell was going on. "I'll be there."

My family home sat as beautiful as ever. The bushes were meticulously trimmed into symmetrical shapes; the lawn was mowed in a checkered pattern, contrasting passes crossing in opposing directions.

Bringing down the floral sculpted brass knocker, I waited for mom to open the door. Moments passed without a response. Worried, I dug out my key and let myself in.

"Mom?" I shouted, my call echoing through the empty house.

Placing the fresh bouquet of flowers on the front entrance table, I tentatively walked through the foyer. I observed the empty formal dining room with a frown. Through the swinging door to the kitchen, the impeccable marble countertops were bare. The room and adjacent breakfast table were empty as well.

A light breeze came in from my left, and I found the patio glass doors were open. Crossing the threshold to the backyard, sprawling flowers and bushes sat undisturbed. I turned to find my mother sitting at the white iron café table. She had a faraway look as she stared into the perfectly manicured flower garden.

"Mom?" She remained unphased, my call unheard. "Mom," I said a little louder as I approached.

She jumped at my voice. "Reid," through surprise, I also read sadness on her face.

"Mom, what's going on?" Panic set in; I was completely unaware of what she had to tell me in person. After our call last night, my mind began to spiral. Did the Dickovers pay a dowry and promise me to Liz? Was I promised at birth? Did my parents and the Dickovers have a blood pact?

"Nothing, dear. Have a seat." She tugged her mouth into a smile, but I noticed the lack of a sparkle in her eye.

Immediately, I knew something must be wrong. She didn't even comment on my lack of a sport jacket. I watched as she wrung her hands and looked on nervously.

"Mom, honestly. You're freaking me out. What's going on?"

"There is something I need to tell you...about your father."

"Dad? Is something wrong with him?"

"Nothing, darling. Nothing...well, maybe a few things. Morally speaking at least." We sat in silence for a few beats as I waited for her to continue. "Your father has had some extramarital relations."

Did she mean cheating? "Do you mean cheating?"

"Well, to put it so curtly, yes." Anger and disgust rolled in my gut. Of the things I expected to hear today, that was not one of them. I balled my fist in an effort to contain my feelings. "He has been involved with a few women over the years, including his assistant at one point."

"A *few*? Mom, I'm—I'm, I'm sorry. What do you need from me? Do you need help leaving?"

She waved a dismissive hand in the air. "No, darling. Nothing like that. I have made my peace with it. It is easier to continue on as is. The reason I am telling you now is," she played with her hair, stalling.

"Well, Bob had been aware of your father's indiscretions for some time. They have a lot of history, as you know. When he discovered the fling between your father and his assistant, he took advantage of the information. You know your father has worked so hard for his partnership in the firm. He helped build the accounting firm to what it is today. That is why we are blessed enough to live the life we live. This home, this garden." She opened her arms to encompass the landscape in front of us. It was gorgeous, a place that would live in my memories forever.

"Bob knows what the firm means to your father," she signed, "to me, and to us. Initially, he wanted to go straight to Heath about the affair, edge out your father and take his place. Your father begged him not to, and in return Bob has requested that your father motion for him to become an equal partner, *and* for you and Elizabeth to marry to secure her future."

My head throbbed at the new information. It made no sense. My dad cheating, and his longest friend blackmailing him, threatening to go to Heath, a managing partner at dad's firm. And...trying to force me into marriage. For Liz's "future"? This wasn't nineteenth century England.

"Her future?" was all I could get out.

She nodded, "we're a respected family name, and you are on the same track to achieve success as your father and Bob. According to

Bob, Elizabeth has not had any promising relationships, and he wants to secure her a marriage."

"Do you realize how fucked up all of this is?"

"Language!"

"Well, mom, I think this situation calls for a little language. You just told me my dad is an adulterer and that you're okay with it. Not to mention, he's being blackmailed by his best friend, the same best friend you want me to willingly make my father-in-law by marrying his awful daughter?"

"You and Elizabeth are childhood friends. I thought you would be open to the idea. That last thing I expected was for you to call her awful." She spoke with disbelief and exasperation. I could hear the desperation in her words.

"Yes, we've been childhood friends by proximity. Sure, she's fun to gossip with at your boring society fundraisers, but she's also rude and entitled."

"Reid, please. Consider it. I am not asking you to understand our marriage, or why I am staying. In fact, I expect you to not understand. However, I do expect you to understand the impact on us it would have if Bob went to the other managing partners with this information. He would likely be pushed out and forced to retire early. Our reputation would also be ruined, our family name would be stained in our social circles. We would have no future here."

"That's a little dramatic," I scoffed. "Dad is two years away from retirement, and you guys are clearly comfortable enough to handle it. You're asking me, your son, your only child, to marry for two more years of work, and preference in social circles. Don't you care what I want?"

"Marrying for convenience is not as terrible as you make it to be. Look at me." A delicate smile appeared, and she motioned to the blooming flowers all around.

"Yeah, mom. Look at you," the words came out a little more disgusted than I intended, "comfortable being disrespected by your husband and asking your child to forego a life of love."

Hurt coated her features, and I immediately regretted my words. My hot temper cooled at the sight of her teary eyes. "Mom, I'm sorry. I didn't mean that." I reached across the table to take her hand in mine. "I didn't mean that at all. I'm just...blindsided. I'm still processing."

"Please, darling. Just think about it," she squeezed my hand in return.

My resolve lessened a little, and I noticed how fragile my mom really was. She was proper and poised, but beneath her perfectly presented persona, I saw a hurt woman. I saw my mom in pain.

Hell, if that wasn't enough to change my mind on the spot. If only it weren't for a certain blonde that kept popping into my mind.

nine

reid

Salsa's, the local downtown Mexican restaurant, was slammed. Their cheap yet delicious lunch special menu always drew a sizeable crowd, especially during the work week.

The festively decorated small restaurant was made even more homey with the local crowd. Brightly painted murals littered the walls, lined with just as vibrant booths. Daisy was distracted every few feet. People who knew her from Slay & Clay were stopping her to say hello, and giving me a cursory glance.

In such a small town, it was an anomaly that we hadn't met yet. Though I swore, familiarity tickled my brain every time I looked at her.

Waiting for someone to take our orders, we settled in the cushy booth seats across from each other. "Thanks for offering to treat me to lunch." Her bright smile was complimented by her sparkling blue eyes.

"Oh, I think there was a misunderstanding. You were treating *me* to lunch as a thank you for giving you the last raspberry tart on Sunday."

She threw a chip from the red plastic basket in the middle of the table, hitting me square in the chest. "That was an apology raspberry tart!"

"Apology? What for?" I asked, curious about how I fucked up again.

"For being a dick when I was a lonely damsel in distress after my shop was robbed."

Her playfulness warmed my heart, and a smile broke through my tough exterior. "Baby, you are anything but a damsel in distress."

Her blue eyes darkened just as they widened at the light nickname. Unsure of where it came from myself, I quickly covered the awkwardness by dousing a chip in salsa.

After ordering—shrimp and rice for her, a chimichanga for me—we talked about everything that floated into our minds. She told me more about Geraldine, the saucy older woman, who handed Liz's ass to her. Her eyes sparkled as she spoke of her progress in sculpting, and they watered with laughter as she reminisced about the time she watched the elderly woman flirt with her college aged employee, Liam. Even though she was very clear that Geraldine was happily married with two kids—Brie and Dane.

"So, numbers boy. Tell me something about the drums. What's your favorite song to play?"

Hands clasped under my chin, I mulled the question over in my mind. "Hmm, maybe 'Come Together' by the Beatles."

"Why?"

"Close your eyes," she raised her eyebrows in question, "humor me. Close those pretty things."

"Fine, but only because you complimented me, and compliments are my life fuel."

"Okay, now imagine the song. Listen to it play in the back of your mind. You hear that intro? The heavy thump accented by the repeating rapid-fire triplets? That's the signature of the song—with it, you don't need to hear anything else to know what song it is. It's simple but innovative, and most importantly, groovy."

"'Groovy'?" she opened one of her now closed eyes.

"I'm in a classic rock cover band. Of course I use words like *groovy*."

"I like it," she said with an affirming nod.

"Speaking of which, we're playing tomorrow night at Street's 7. If you're interested in watching."

"Ellie and I were planning on it," she offered a big smile that made me excited to see someone else excited to see my play.

My parents still had no idea about my hobby. Though it was a small town, the circles sometimes ran smaller. At least when it came to what mom's crowd deemed themselves as high society. Well, as "high society" as you could get in suburban Pennsylvania.

I insisted on walking her back to her shop, which I immediately regretted as I thought back to my conversation with my mother yesterday. Still unsure where I stood, I was leaning towards honoring them and settling with Liz. If anything, I was still undecided, and it was unfair to give Daisy any other impression.

Though it was a friendly lunch, as we stopped outside her shop entrance, she turned to me. The lunch was friendly, but there was obviously a tension in the air when we were alone. She looked at my mouth, her lips parted, and I wanted to kiss her. I did. *Not until I figured out what to do about Liz.*

Raising a hand, I took a step back and gave her a small wave. As I retreated to my car, I silently hated myself. Her confused expressions both humored and hurt me.

"See ya' tomorrow."

ten

daisy

"His loss," I whispered to myself as I shaped the vase in front of me.

I wasn't sure what a certain sexy drummer's problem was, but I had my own shit to deal with. The signals he'd been sending me had been so mixed, I felt no more stable than the lump of clay I was working on. *What the hell was I making, anyway?*

Frustrated, I groaned. No way was I going to let a guy put me in an artistic slump. It was fine if he wasn't into me. I was a damn prize, and I knew it. But the least he could do was let a girl know.

Instead, he showed up with pastries two mornings in a row. Fueled with confidence and the way he looked at me with those steely grays, I asked him to lunch. Then, at said lunch, he asked me to watch his show tonight. *Signals of interest, am I right?*

And yet, when he walked me home, despite proceeding to stare at my scrumptious mouth with his sexy eyes, he did...nothing. Nada. Zilch.

The sound of the front door brought me back to the present. "Elle's back here!" I called my best friend to the back room and made a mental note to swipe through Dately later.

"What is that?" Ellie stared at my wheel in confusion. I tilted my head and mimicked her expression.

"I'm not quite sure, it just spoke to me." *Lies*. But no way was I going to tell her about Reid. What was there to even tell her?

"I'm thinking...an abstract vase? See, a flower can be placed right here." I pointed to a hole atop a curve of the vase and smiled to myself. "I'm gonna place this on the pottery rack and clean up, then we can go. Give me like ten minutes, max."

Distracted by a recent creation ready for firing—an ornate cowboy boot vase—I held up two glaze options. "Elle's, that cowboy boot I sent you a picture of is ready to be glazed. What d'ya think?"

Smiling like a dope at her phone, Ellie was distracted. I'd bet five dollars and a Swirly Pop truffle she was smiling at Theo.

I called her attention. "Did you hear anything I said?"

"Yeah, totally. Um, green."

"Green? Have you lost your mind?" I slammed the containers on the counter and snatched her phone. "What is distracting you from giving sound advice?"

"Hey!" she protested. Ellie's green-eyed hunk filled the screen. He smiled, his face drenched in sweat. Ha. I'd tell Ellie later she owed me five bucks and a Swirly Pop truffle.

"Those pretty green eyes," I sighed. "Damnit Ellie, if you don't want to ride him, I will."

I was joking, of course. That man was wrapped up in Ellie. Which he should be. Anyone would be crazy to not realize how amazing of a person Ellie was. All the same, I would welcome a distraction from my life—not Theo, though. Just to be clear.

The calls from Carl were still a regular occurrence, and I'd sweetly talked Kendrick, the cop assigned to my break-in, into helping me build a case for a protection order. My mom was also still MIA since stealing from me. Luckily, Reid helped me fix the financial problem, but the personal one cut to my core. I knew my mother to be many things, but never did I expect her to stoop that low.

Reid was the only person in my life to know about the situation, and that was because he'd happened upon me talking to Officer Lawson. I hadn't even told Ellie yet, and I wasn't sure that I would. I rarely spoke about my mom for a reason; I liked to keep that part of my life far away.

Being the nosey and overbearing friend I was, I clicked through Ellie's messages. The sweet-talking Bucky Barnes look alike from Wild Cider was asking when they'd be seeing each other again. "Oh, Graham wants to see you again?"

After her first stage performance, Graham promptly hit Ellie on. As she should be. My best friend deserved the world; she deserved a partner who didn't cheat and told her how pretty and nice and smart and amazing she was. She also deserved to play a little, have a little fun. She sure as shit wasn't going to make it happen for herself, so I had to step in.

Fueled by that, and a little mischief building inside of me wanting to blow off steam, I responded for her.

Ellie

> Hopefully soon, but first I need to know. What are your intentions? I hope they're bad ;)

Promptly, he responded to scheduling a date with her next weekend. Point Daisy. I still had it. If Reid couldn't see that, then that was on him. I still had a field to play.

"What does this mean?" Ellie asked.

"What does this mean?" I echoed her question. "This means shopping! But first, nachos."

For the second time in forty-eight hours, I gorged myself on the complimentary chips and salsa. Being that this was girls' night, though, we also had a round of margaritas.

Weakly walking out of the Mexican restaurant with our bloated bellies, we were in high spirits. There was no one I loved more than my sweet, practical, and kind best friend. This was the best kind of date night.

"Where to?" Ellie asked, probably hoping I had forgotten my earlier claim of needing to go shopping for her date with Graham.

"Honey & Co." Pulling her along, we stood in front of the display window of one of my favorite stores. Lingerie. See through lace and carefully placed satin was such a simple pleasure.

"Daisy, is lingerie shopping something we should really do after having just gorged ourselves with nachos?"

"Not 'we,' *you*. For your date next Saturday. Besides, the Assets don't go on for another hour. We have time to kill. Let's find you something irresistible."

Inside, the associate pointed out new arrivals when my phone pinged from my bag. Hoping it was either an update from Kendrick or a text from Reid, Sandy's name flashed across the screen.

Sandy

> Sry for everything hon. Can I come back? I want 2 apologize.

> I have nowhere else 2 go. It won't happen again.

I cursed under my breath, anger rising to the surface. Either she ignored the list of women's shelters I snuck into her bag, or she'd been kicked out of them. If I was a betting woman, I'd wager the latter.

My heart ached first at knowing she was in need again, but my feelings of anger quickly took over when I realized that was the only reason she wanted to apologize. I had worked so hard for what I had, and it meant nothing to her than another way to manipulate and use me.

Not anymore.

Daisy

You're not welcome here any longer. Unless you have the 3k you stole from me, don't bother coming around. I filed a police report.

"You okay, Daze?" Ellie called after me, concerned.

"Peachy," I forced a smile. This night was about Ellie. Not me. "Now, what do we have here?" Directing her to a lacy two-piece, I pushed my hurt and disappointment down.

"Daze, seriously. Is everything okay?"

"Just Sandy." I lifted my shoulder in a shrug, trying to remain nonchalant. Ellie knew crumbs of my past I had left her, but not the entire story. I preferred to keep it that way. I didn't need pity, and I didn't need judgement. I just needed my people; people I could trust and count on.

"Sandy? As in your mom, Sandy? Again?"

"Yes, but it's nothing. We're here for *you*. I'm not letting you get out of doing something for yourself."

After a little more pep-talking, Ellie walked out with the sexy black set. Point Daisy, again. Damn, I was on a roll. I even treated myself to a few new pairs of lace thongs that were on sale.

Walking out of Honey & Co., two familiar faces greeted us. "Jake!" I shouted cheerfully. "Where's Penny? Hi Theo!" Ellie's crush that she refused to admit, Theo, was with his best friend. Having met the fun couple, Jake and Penny, at Wild Cider, I now considered them friends as well.

"Daisy!" Jake lifted me in a big, friendly hug, followed by Theo. "Penny ran ahead to grab us a table top a bit ago. Theo and I made a pit stop at Swirly Pop."

Theo held up the signature bubblegum pink bag of the local hand-made candy shop. "I had to grab some cranberry truffles for my mom. They're her favorite and there's a good chance I would be disowned if I showed up to family movie night without a box."

"I see you've been doing some shopping, too." Jake motioned to our matching velvety black bags.

"You know it. Next time we'll make sure Penny is with us," I winked. "You should see what Ellie snagged-ow!" Ellie stepped on my toes, made even worse by the fact that I was wearing open-toed shoes.

"I'm just gonna put this in my car...I'll meet you at Street 7." Ellie ran off, and Theo quickly followed.

Jake and I stood side by side, staring after them.

"He has it so bad for her," his best friend confessed.

"I know, but so does she. I caught her staring at a picture of him on her phone earlier. Smiling like a sap."

Chuckling, we began walking towards Street 7 together, stopping off at Slay & Clay to drop-off my new goodies.

"So, I hear you have an admirer," Jake prodded.

"I have many," I joked. "Please, clarify."

"A certain drummer?"

Doing my best to hide my surprise, I hummed. "Hmmm...not ringing a bell."

"Sure. Just tell the certain drummer, who you have no idea about, thank you for saving us a table." I looked at him, my eyebrows raised in silent question. Noting my expression, he chuckled to himself before explaining. "When Penny got there, there were no tables, except one. At the front. The guitar chick from the band told us it was reserved for Daisy."

"Kara, she plays the bass," I corrected. "And are you sure she said Daisy? Not Ellie?"

"One hundo. The guitar chick—"

"–Kara."

"*Kara* specifically said the drummer saved it for Daisy."

"Huh." *Interesting. Very interesting.*

Entering the overly crowded bar, we wove our way through groups and pairs, happily drinking, dancing, and talking. At the front, Penny sat alone at a tabletop. Focused on the black-haired, gray eyed, dreamy drummer, I ignored Jake and Penny making kissy faces at each other. My stupid heart fluttered at the quick smirk he gave me right before his head banged into a drum solo.

"'Not ringing a bell,' my ass," Jake leaned in and whispered in my ear.

I held up my middle finger in response.

Reid finished his drum solo with a flourish, and I cheered with the crowd. A few women had made their way into the small open floor area and were shooting swoony eyes in the drummers' direction. Again, he kept his eyes on me, and *was that a smolder?*

I felt the thump of the drum, followed by the quick symbol taps, and an instant smile lit up my face. His favorite song to play. In a trance, I began nodding to the beat and with a silent look I knew he knew I knew the meaning.

Ellie filled the empty seat next to me, but my eyes remained transfixed on the stage. "Apparently, the drums in this song are iconic," I shouted, acknowledging Ellie's arrival. "I see it now."

"Where'd you hear that?"

If I pulled my eyes from the stage, I was sure I would have caught her staring at me like I had two heads. I tried to keep my tone as neutral as possible. "Reid mentioned it was one of his favorite songs to play."

Thankfully, Ellie didn't probe further. She was distracted with her own situation in the form of Theo Emerson standing at her back.

For the night, I could keep my secrets. One being the man on stage. The other being the text response from my mom I was working so hard to ignore.

eleven

reid

Daisy

What do you think?

ATTACHED TO THE TEXT was a picture of...something. Atop of a messy workstation was a sculpture, I assumed, of a man's face. His face displayed a noticeable contrast, with half of it being perfectly proportioned. The beautifully sculpted side boasted a chiseled jawline, defined cheekbones, and a single tranquil eye. The other half was that same man but covered with protruding knobs and bumps and jagged shapes, with a single, wild, excited eye.

Reid

I think many things. Like how water isn't wet, and how people always disagree with me, but they're wrong.

Daisy

What?

Reid

Wet means something is saturated with a liquid, water itself is a liquid. It's not wet, but it can make things wet.

Daisy

Is this some sort of sexual thing? What's going on here?

What was going on was I was trying to avoid answering her question about her sculpture.

Daisy

Are you trying to avoid talking about my
sculpture?

Reid

That's what that was?

Daisy

Ha. Ha.

A few clicks on my phone and a ringing sound filled the receiver.

"Well, well, well. Hey butt head," Daisy's cheery voice filtered through with an undertone of scolding. Leaning back in my chair, I spoke low as to keep our conversation in the confines of my office.

"Butt head? That's a bit harsh."

"Why do you sound like that? All gravely and sexy like?"

"There you go again, calling me sexy." I felt her laughter through the phone and realized I was smiling, myself. Like a big dope. My phone vibrated against my ear, and I pulled it away to see *Mom* flash across the screen.

Memories of our lunch conversation from two weeks before rushed back as I hit the decline button. Yes, I'd thought more about the situation. No, I didn't have an answer. But there was a voice within me that warned I'd inevitably end up doing my duty as a son and go along with it. Resentment filled me as I listened to the laughter of the girl who'd lit up my world, knowing that we would never be more.

My eyes drifted to the framed picture next to my large computer monitor. Mom and dad had their arms around twenty-four-year-old me. In my cap and grown, I was so proud of myself for completing my Masters. The crow's feet at the corner of my mother's eyes were a reminder of all the times she smiled for me. Cheered me on.

She had always been there for me. In her own way at times, sure, but she was always there. It was my turn to do the same.

Guilt hit me like a freight train, replacing the once felt resentment towards my mom, knowing who was on the other side of this phone call. What I wanted to do was take Daisy on a date, lean into all the flirting, and live on the dangerous side her smile beckoned me to. What I felt I had to do was back off, call my mom back and tell her my decision, then swallow my pride and apologize to Liz. Being it'd been a few weeks now since the pottery date night, I had to reach out sooner rather than later.

I cleared my throat. "I was calling to hear more about your sculpture, but if you'd rather talk about how attractive I am, we can do that instead." *Shit*. Okay, the flirting stopped now.

"I don't know if you deserve to hear how hot you are after evading a discussion about my art." I paused for fear of how I would respond. "Since you asked," she continued, "the sculpture is inspired by you."

"Me?"

"Yes, you. The two sides of you are so contrasting, yet they fit together in a way that is beautiful. Speaking of two sides, are you a Gemini by chance?"

"Gemini?"

"Never mind," she brushed off, "any-who-dle, on one side you are strong, methodical, and stoic. On the other, you're spunky."

"Spunky?"

"Spunky. That's the best word, I think. A little of bada-bing bada-bang, some rat-a-tat-tat."

This woman. I had no idea what she was saying, but I would have been fine to sit and listen to her talk like this for hours. I pictured her with a little bit of clay in her hair and flecked across her forehead from a session of inspired sculpting. If I were there, I'd watch her flail her arms to punctuate each word with wild eyes of her own.

"Ah. Baba-bing, bada-bang? Why didn't you say so?" I asked.

"Reid Fletcher Bartholomew, don't tease me now."

"Reid Malcom Flores," I corrected. "And I'm not teasing."

"Flores? As in flowers? That's funny. My last name is Bloom. As in flowers."

"Interesting." It was interesting. How our names both echoed flowers. What was more interesting was her first name being Daisy. With a name like that, you'd think she'd be better suited as a florist. For her nature, though, pottery was just right.

Her carefreeness and kindness worked together to put beauty in the world.

"Lot's a of one-word responses from you today, Reid Malcom Flores."

"Sorry, it's been pretty hectic at work. Those numbers have been giving me the runaround. Well, thank you for creating something inspired by me. That might be the most thoughtful thing anyone has ever done for me."

"When are we going to hang out again?" She sounded hopeful, and my stomach knotted at the anticipation in her voice.

"Um, not sure right now. We have another show at Wild Cider on Saturday?"

"Oh," she sounded like she saw the hidden meaning, that she knew I was now trying to create some distance. "Okay, sounds good. See you then."

Before I could explain, she ended the call and silence hung on the other end.

It was hard to focus the rest of the day. The numbers and accounts and invoices blurred; it was all nonsense. I wasn't sure what was more frustrating. That numbers, the one thing I could always rely on to be consistent, made little sense, or that I felt immediate regret when I blew Daisy off.

Sitting in my car at the end of the day, I closed my eyes and rested my head against the back of the seat. Having not left the parking lot yet, I commanded my car to dial *Mom*.

"Reid, sweetheart. How is your day?" my mother's light voice filled the car, with a hint of concern.

"Hey mom. It's alright. How is yours?"

"Better now that you've returned my call. If I didn't know any better, I'd venture to guess you declined my call earlier."

"Yes, I was working. I'm calling back now, though." I took a deep breath, steadying my nerves. If I didn't do it now, I knew I'd run to Daisy and never look back. With my heart in my stomach, I took the plunge. "I've thought about our discussion the other day."

"Is that so?" her voice was steady, but I knew her, and I knew she was trying to manage her tone.

"I—I'll do it."

Silence hung thickly between us. I half expected her to tell me to hell with it. Let my dad fall. "Oh, alright," she responded mater-of-factly, and I felt a pang in my chest. "Well, thank you, dear. That...well, I can't quite explain to you what that means to me."

"Love you, mom."

"Love you, my dear son," I heard emotion catch in her breath. Mom was never really one for emotions. I'd only seen her cry the one time I got a concussion during a football game. Other than that, it was always all smiles. Sometimes, robotic smiles. She quickly recovered by clearing her throat. "I better get an invitation out to Bob and Elaine for dinner. Oh! I can make that lovely sea bass recipe from Martha Stewart."

Whatever emotion I felt from my mom was instantly taken over with dinner party planning. Inwardly, I groaned at the idea of sitting around a table with my parents and the Dickover's. Nothing felt more uncomfortable than having to pretend to not to know of my dad's shitty transgressions, or Bob's disgusting blackmail, while I sat across from them eating sea bass.

"Sounds great. I'll talk to you later."

twelve

daisy

"Hey, you okay out there?" Calley called from the back. "Carl again?"

"Yes," I said, defeated. Leaning on the counter, I covered my face in my hands. The exhaustion was overwhelming, and I just wished he would stop calling. With a heavy sigh, I rubbed at my face in frustration. If the WWE worthy slam I gave the phone didn't break it, I could think of a hundred other ways to do so.

The sound of Calley's gum popping approached. "What're you gonna do?"

"Update Kendrick...again."

"The cute cop guy?"

"That's the one. Let this be a lesson," I wagged my finger like a teacher enciting epiphanies in her students, "take shit from no one. Also, learn how to block numbers on a landline."

"I can almost guarantee I will never use a landline again once I leave here," the teen snorted.

"Yeah, yeah, you kids and your technology. You sure you're good alone tonight?"

"There's only four people registered tonight; I should be fine. And Brody is going to come by halfway through so he can stay with me through close and walk me home." Calley referenced her teenage heartthrob boyfriend. Ah, to be young again and love boys with unironic mullets.

"Good. Also, I hired a new gal, Polly. She starts training on Monday."

When I called the local rehabilitation center with my job ad, they had Polly on standby for recommendation, which was always promising. Liam had been gone for a few weeks now, and I'd yet to find a replacement. Ellie had been amazing enough to help me when things were too crazy, but my best friend needed her life back. Especially if her weekend trip with Theo went as well as I hoped it had.

After making sure Calley was prepped and ready for her pottery painting night, I went upstairs to slip into something more...inspired.

I was an optimist. Not stupid. Reid was blowing me off, and that was just fine. But that didn't mean I wasn't going to make it hard for him. Honestly, how rude of him to give me all these signals—taking me to lunch, the flirty texts, the lingering looks—just to suddenly shut me out.

Fingering through my closet, I landed on a lilac-colored sheer tank and a deep purple floor length tiered skirt. Under the sheer tank, I wore a lace bra in the same deep purple as the skirt. My trusty nipple covers did the lord's work, hiding the forbidden goods. This outfit was good for one of two things—ripping off, or totally averting your gaze. I walked to Wild Cider, wondering which option Reid would choose.

The Assets were just arriving when I waltzed through the front doors. I knew I was early, but I wanted time to trap—I meant, say hi to—Reid. Also, I was a sucker for Wild Ciders brisket fries and fried pickles.

Sitting pretty at the same front table as last time, I cozy'd up to my baskets of fried goodness. Mid-bite, a familiar voice called my name. With a swift, hungry girl move, I stuffed a fried pickle drenched in house made ranch in my mouth. Turning, I watched Brian make his way down from the stage. He pulled me into a half hug before sitting across from me and stealing a fry.

"If you're gonna steal a fry, at least make it worth it and get some brisket in that bite."

Obeying, he picked up several fries coated in beef and barbecue. Licking his fingers clean, he gave me a once over. "Lookin' awfully pretty today, Daisy. It wouldn't be for a certain drummer, would it?"

"Now, now, Brian. If I didn't know you were married, I'd think you were hitting on me." I innocently batted my lashes.

"Not a chance," he laughed. "I just know a flirty outfit when I see one." Saying nothing, we locked our eyes and engaged in what I would describe as a staring contest.

"Ha! You blinked!"

Confused, he looked at me. "Yeah, that's kind of a human thing. You wouldn't know anything about it." I threw a fry at him before popping another fried pickle into my mouth. "Speaking of drummer boy, look alive."

As he stood, he gave me a curt nod and called out a greeting to Reid behind me. Using all my willpower, I kept my gaze on my artery clogging food. *For the love of all things good, do not turn around.*

"Daisy?" Reid's gruff voice was close behind.

Doing my best nonchalant over-the-shoulder look, I gave a flirty smile. "Hey handsome. Come here often?"

A multitude of emotions crossed his face. I tried making sense of them, but couldn't decide where to land. Was that excitement? Anger? Hurt? Resentment? Pain?

"You're a bit early, aren't you?" Stopping in front of me, a cart stacked with round shaped travel cases squeaked to a halt. While I couldn't make sense of his emotions a moment ago, the lust that clouded his eyes was clear as day.

Blow me off now, hotshot.

My body felt on fire under the weight of his gaze.

"A little, but I was hoping to steal a few moments of your time to say hi. Hi." I said and gave a small wave.

"Hi," he replied. The clatter of glasses and the chatter of the few patrons filled the air while we were locked in in our own little world.

"Fried pickle?" I asked, breaking the spell. He held up a toned hand and shook his head, declining. I bit my tongue, willing myself to stay quiet as he clearly struggled with what he wanted to say next.

He repositioned his hands on the handle of the cart and motioned his head towards the stage. "Walk with me?"

There was something in his words and movement. Something unsaid was hiding in him. Nerves tickled me in anticipation of what the words might be as my intuition warned that there was danger up ahead. Frankly, it was his problem if he couldn't speak up.

Standing, I left my food and a light sweater I brought, to keep claim of the primo seats. Walking up and keeping in stride, I walked alongside him, pretending not to notice the sidelong glances he shot my way. Smugly, I kept quiet.

"You look great," he said. "Purple is your color. Then again, you're the only person I've ever met who regularly wears every color known to man. Actually, I can confidently say every color is your color."

"Well, thanks." I blushed. Quickly, he changed the subject, and we each rambled about our week. Rounding the sage, we stopped behind a large speaker, the height of it covering us.

"I would have beat that goose too, if I wasn't deadly afraid of them." Reid said, exasperated.

Bent over from laughter, I wiped a tear from my eye. "You? Big, bad, practical, Reid. Scared of geese?"

"Listen, until you've been bitten by one, I don't want to hear it."

"You've been bitten by a goose?" my voice reached new decibels as I failed to conceal my laughter.

The badass bass player came in from my peripheral. "Oh, is this the goose story?" She shook her head. "Reid, you got to get over it, man. I'm Kara," the bold red-haired bass player stuck out her hand.

"Daisy," I introduced, accepting her outstretched hand. Reid had told me many stories of Kara and his role as resident wing-man, but I was finally getting to meet her in person. She presented herself with a swagger, the kind that I hoped to embody. Oh yeah, I could totally see how she would be a player.

"Cute," she flashed the playful smile Reid told me of.

"Keep it in your pants. She's not interested." Reid huffed with a roll of his eyes.

"Can't knock a girl for trying," she laughed. "Well, I see you're busy here. Want me to get your drums set up so you can finish up?"

Reid gratefully accepted, stepping aside to pass the reigns of the cart to his bandmate. We watched as Kara disappeared, pushing the cart.

"Okay, now I have to hear the whole goose-pocalypse story." I prodded.

"Goose-pocalypse. I'm stealing that. So, when I was seven, my grandpa took me fishing. I was so excited. I was running with my clumsy kid legs and barreled down the hill. Unable to stop myself, I crashed into some bushes. Apparently, there was a goose nest there, and apparently, geese hate humans near their babies. The son-of-a-bitch bit me. Gave me a scar. Now every time I see the scar, I relive the horror."

My laughter ceased as Reid lifted his shirt, unveiling taunt muscles. Tall and lean, his stomach was defined, his pecs shapely. And there was that deep V I had caught a glimpse of that paint and sip night. Now, I knew him as more than that. I knew him as a dynamic and caring person. The feelings I'd been building for him worked with his body to do cruel things to me, teasing me further as the V dipped below his waistline.

A white scar sat on his right pec, and I reached out to stroke it gently.

Sparks flew as our skin connected. Silently, I hoped Kara was somewhere nearby to help put out the fire. We were right on track to have an emergency situation; if the sparks didn't do it, my panties would—I wouldn't have put it past them to spontaneously combust at the feel of his tight muscle. His breath hitched at my touch and his brow furrowed as he surveyed where my finger traced.

He placed a firm hand over mine, holding it to his chest. Slowly, he raked his gaze over me. A trail of heat flowed up my arm, over my neck, and landed on my lips.

Stepping forward, I moved my other hand around his neck. At his six foot five, he stood over a foot taller than my five foot three. Pulling him down, I raised onto my toes, and sweetly, softly, brought our lips together.

We didn't have a chance to break before he opened his mouth to me, and I followed. Happily, I brought his tongue into my mouth, taking turns between sucking and biting his bottom lip. The world around me faded, and I was lost in him. His scent. His taste. His sounds.

Then he pulled away.

Taking a wide step back, he brushed a hand through his hair. I stared at him with wide eyes and almost wanted to whimper. Being flustered looked so sexy on him.

"That can't happen again," he said, gesturing between us.

"Sure, it can," I purred, taking a step towards him. He dropped his head and whispered, barely audible. "What was that?"

"There's something I need to tell you." He repeated, lifting his head. With the look of a wounded puppy, his eyes avoided mine.

Nervously, I laughed. "You're not going to tell me you're married or something, are you?" The solemn look on his face did nothing to soothe my worries. "Oh. My. God. You're married."

"No," he shook his head. "But I will be soon."

"You're engaged?" Somehow, that felt worse. Maybe because it was coming from him now, as a fact, and yet he never said anything. Unless...he did? Did he? No, I swore he didn't. "Then what is this between us? I know I haven't been imagining it."

"It's—no, I'm not engaged either. It's complicated." He ran a shaky hand through his hair again, a nervous tick. "You haven't been imagining this. I have a lot going on right now, and I've been trying to figure out what to do. You were so unexpected, and I've been enjoying getting to know you so much. I didn't want it to end."

"Wow," I laughed, partly in disgust, partly in disbelief. "Well, don't let me keep you from your fiancé. I am so glad I could help you with your decision. Have a nice life."

Turning, I stomped off. I had a lot going on too, but you didn't see me going around flirting and kissing people while being in some weird relationship. I wanted to yell at him, maybe throw my shoe.

A cacophony of instrumental sounds started up as the band began testing their instruments and tuning. Reid cursed from behind me and gripped my arm just as I rounded the stage. "Daisy, please. Give me a chance to explain."

I ripped my arm from him with a disappointed grin. "No, thanks."

"I'm begging for one minute, please. I promise I didn't mean for this to happen. My family is going through a bit of a crisis, and this is how I can help. I need to do my part to support my family."

"Reid, in case you haven't noticed, I'm having a bit of a family crisis myself. Although, I'm sure you have noticed given you were there when the cops were taking my statement after my own mother robbed me, and when her crazy ex called to threaten me. And yet, this has all been real to me." My hands were flailing now, and my words dripped with anger.

"Well, maybe your lack of family is why you can't understand why it's so important to me to help mine." There it was. My biggest insecurity. My biggest secret. My biggest fear. And he laid it all out in front of me.

"What an incredibly awful way to kick me while I'm down," I blinked quickly to hold back the tears. I didn't cry. No, I moved on, took care of myself, and made things work.

"Reid, come on man," Brian called from the stage, waving my sparing opponent over.

Aggressively, he rubbed his face, and I hated that the look of his pain made my heart hurt. "I didn't mean that. I'm sorry. Can we just—can we talk about this later?"

"Don't bother." Turning, I took a deep breath and stilled my shoulders.

At the table, Jake and Penny now sat, sipping their ciders. Further into the crowd, I saw Theo and Ellie making their way over.

On cue, to make the spectacularly awful day worse, I received a text.

Sandy

> Daisy found a new place 2 stay. Can u send me $100? I don't get paid til Wed

Sighing, I decided to make the best of this. Turn my own mood around. I looked hot as shit in my purple get-up. It would be a shame to let it go to waste.

Opening my banking app, I transferred my mom $200.

Daisy

> Sent you some money. You still owe me my 3k btw.

Sauntering over to my friends, I heard a small round of applause come from the group.

"Hey, what are we clapping..." I asked, running up. Following their stares, my eyes settled on my best friend's hand joined with Theo's. "Ah, the royal couple making their first public appearance." I gave a facetious bow and joined the clapping.

"Technically, yesterday was our first public appearance," Theo drew her in closer, lazily but possessively putting his arm around her shoulders. And damn if I wasn't a little jealous. "She met my family yesterday."

Ah, there was that word again. *Family.*

"Oh, serious," Penny said, wiggling her brows.

"As serious as it gets." He placed a kiss on Ellie's head just as Brian called her name from the stage.

She gave an apologetic smile to the group and turned to Theo. "That's my cue!"

I watched as he pulled her in for a kiss and they stared lovingly at each other. I hoped this jealous self-loathing thing would subside quickly.

"Save it for the bedroom, you horn dogs." I teased, throwing a fried pickle at them.

They broke apart and my superstar best friend made her way to the stage with the band where the king, Asshole Reid, joined them.

thirteen

reid

> I want to apologize. How does ice cream and groveling sound?

MY FINGER HOVERED OVER the *send* button. The sound of ice cream made my already uncomfortable stomach turn even more. Groveling didn't sound like me in the least, and I sure as hell didn't want to apologize. Nor did I think I should.

If there was one person who deserved my apology, it was Daisy. Unfortunately, if there was one person I shouldn't talk to right now, it was probably Daisy.

Erasing the message with a sigh, I drafted a new one and hit send.

> Are you free for dessert this evening?

> Only if you're the dessert, and you preface with an apology.

I swallowed back the bile that rose in my throat.

> That was my intention. Pick you up at seven?

Liz

> Good. See you then.

Rolling over, I covered my head with a pillow. Unsure how I was going to stomach this evening, I knew I would have to figure it out eventually. I couldn't very well marry a woman without at least figuring out how to enjoy her company.

It was true we'd grown up together, but that was just because our dads were best friends. She was always there. Which gave me plenty of time to notice how she was always taking digs at other girls. She was snarky and entitled, and there was nothing I disliked more.

Actually, there was one thing I disliked more. Being at the mercy of the direction of other people. That was the one thing I'd been working my adult life to get away from, and here I was again. Still a pawn in my parents' social game.

As if I summoned her, a call came in from my mom. Groaning, I answered the call, the pillow still on my face.

"Good morning," my voice was muffled by the inches of memory foam I typically slept on for my neck.

"Reid, I did not understand a word you just said. Enunciate please." Mom had a special talent for making everything sound like the most important thing in the world, but that she couldn't be bothered with it at the same time.

I removed the pillow with a grunt. "Good. Morning. Mother."

"Ah, much better," she said smugly. "I'm calling to invite you to dinner tonight. The Dickovers will be joining."

"I have plans with Liz."

"Elizabeth? Delightful! What time?"

"I'm picking her up at seven for dessert."

"That's perfect!" Her excitement showed that either she didn't hear my disinterest, or that she did and didn't care. "Come have dinner. Five sharp. Then you two can go out for dessert."

A carefree blonde popped into my head with flashes of her pink highlights. Forcefully, I had to shake her from my mind. My fate was sealed, my mind made up. Was it too late to go back?

I rolled my eyes. "Yep, sounds great. Thanks mom."

"See you then, dear. Love you!"

"This is delicious, Carrey. What is it again? You must share the recipe," Elaine Dickover crooned, making hearts appear in my mom's eyes at the praise.

"Oh! It's roasted sea bass. Martha Stewart shared the recipe on the Morning Show. I knew I had to make it for your visit." *Kiss ass.* "I'll send you the link."

A tap against my foot irritated me, knowing in my gut what, or should I say *who*, it was. Shifting in my seat, I tried to put more physical space around me and the others. Moments later, I felt another tap and clenched my jaw in frustration. Peering down, a sock wearing, heel clad foot was attempting to rub up my shin.

Across the table, Liz sat with a smirk and sent me a wink. I shied away as best as I could, causing her to have to scoot further down into her seat to continue grazing me. The slump it put her in was comical. As I looked at her with a raised brow, she straightened in her chair. I returned her gesture with a tight-lipped smile. Shifting my feet again, I made sure to place them out of reach beneath my seat.

"So sorry to ruin your evening plans, Reid." Elaine directed her attention to me. Her short stature and dark hair were echoed in her daughter. Keeping the grays showing—a rebellious move in her social circle—Elaine liked to wear a voluminous short bob. Her hair practically vibrated with her excitement.

"I assure you; nothing has been ruined," I mustered as much politeness as possible. "I was just going to take Liz for ice cream after, if that is alright with you?"

"Of course! That would be fabulous."

Conversation carried on, but nothing registered as I sat in silence, pushing around the last half of my fish and sweet potatoes.

"Reid?" dad's commanding voice called from the head of the table. I lifted my head to meet his gaze with a questioning grunt. "Bob asked if you saw the closing numbers for the day."

"Oh, sorry. No, not yet. Good, I hope?" I used my only working brain cell to form a question. The fog of what had led to this point, what I had to let go, consumed me. I was really in no position to talk about the stock exchange right now. Nor did I care.

"Turbo closed out at just about $169, a twenty-seven percent hike. I would say that's pretty good." His hackle would have been considered chuffed any other day, but knowing who he was as a person made it sound diabolical. "It's only going to go up from here." Referencing his latest prediction that the electric car company was going to do well, he looked pleased with himself.

I wondered if he blackmailed his way into that as well. Maybe insider trading?

"That's great, Mr. Dickover." Though I couldn't be more disinterested, I gave my best effort at a smile. Instead, it came out tight lipped in a way that I figured was my permanent smile now.

Thankfully, dad took back over the conversation, and they began going back and forth about the latest projections. Elaine, Liz, and mom were talking in hushed tones about the latest gossip—the Garrison's pending divorce. While they mulled over who would get the country club membership, I couldn't escape the sinking feeling in my gut.

Was this to be my life from now on? Was this a glimpse of my future? The stock market, gossip, and Martha Stewart recipes?

My jaw ached, causing me to realize I was grinding my teeth. I needed out of this room. Tugging at my collar that was suddenly too tight, the table shook as I stood abruptly. Wide eyes greeted me around the table.

"Liz, ready to go?" I offered.

She answered the question with a sickly sweet smile and a nod. Gracefully, she met me at the front door.

"Couldn't wait another moment," Elaine giggled softly. "Love is in the air."

Something was in the air, but I didn't have the balls to tell her it was shame and disappointment that hung heavily in my glances towards my parents.

fourteen

reid

THE BRIGHTLY LIT LOOP & Scoop greeted us with a cheery bell at the opening of the door. We walked across the pink and white checkered flooring and stared into the clear casing. Gallons of signature flavors sat for the picking.

"Small More O'Smores please," I placed my order with the tall, gangly man, hiding slick hair under a paper boat shaped hat. Motioning for Liz to order, I briskly paid, and we stepped to the side.

The worker handed over our bowls—More O'Smores for me, plain vanilla with sprinkles for Liz—and the cheery tune of the bell sang again. The man behind the case let out a heavy sigh that held a story.

"Hey Daze," surely, he didn't mean Daze as in Daisy. As in my Daisy. Unprepared to see her again, I hoped with all my vigor that it wasn't her.

"Stuart little, hello dear friend," yep, that was her. "It's been a rough week. Hit me with the usual."

My back straightened and stiffened, and my shoes suddenly became cemented. I hadn't noticed Liz take a seat at a cracked turquoise booth along the side wall.

"Reid, aren't you coming?" she called after me. *Shit.*

"Reid?" Daisy asked from behind. Slowly, I turned to face her.

"Hey, uh, Daisy. You look...good." She looked better than good. Her hair was knotted atop her head, golden and pink stained strands falling every which way. Her clothes—an oversized shirt hanging over one shoulder and flowing green pants—covered her delicately. Paint speckled her all over, whispers of her creative spirit.

Though she quickly transformed her face, I caught hurt cross it for a brief moment. Had I blinked, I would have missed it.

Looking at me, she ignored my comment. Nodding to my cup of ice cream, she nodded. "Good taste"

"Huh?"

She pointed to my cup. "More O'Smores, my favorite." On cue, Stuart handed a chocolate dipped cone with three scoops of the treat filled ice cream to Daisy. "Good God, Stu. Trying to put me in a sugar coma?"

"You said it was a rough week," he shrugged. "It's on me."

"Wow, there really is hope for you yet." She gave him an appraising nod that told me there was more to their friendship. "Thanks Stuart."

She gave him a genuine, friendly, bright smile and I wished for nothing more than for her to direct one of those towards me.

"Life is too short to waste it eating vanilla ice cream. You gotta go for the good stuff." She took a long lick up the side of the cone. I watched as her tongue flattened against the chocolate coating, gathering the dripping liquid. My brain short-circuited as I watched her pull her mouth away, only to lick at the corner of her lips. A small moan of pleasure escaped her lips, coaxing me to grow a semi.

Too many dirty things crossed my mind. Was that what she would sound like with my mouth on her? The way she licked up the ice cream...I couldn't help but picture it was my cock.

"Well, have fun with your date." Her voice pulled me from my lust filled haze as she looked over my shoulder at Liz. Meeting my gaze, we had an unspoken conversation. I knew she was judging me for being with the woman who was so rude to her on the date night where our story started.

That story, though, was now over.

I watched her silently as she walked back out onto the sidewalk and disappeared in the direction of her shop.

"Hey man, you're drooling," Stuart said from behind the case. "And I don't think it's the ice cream. You might want to get back to your girl over there."

Clawing my way out of the fog, I turned back to Liz. Taking a seat across from her, we ate in silence. With the grace of a young woman who surely graduated etiquette school, she took small proper bites of her ice cream. Vanilla, the butt of Daisy's ice cream judgment. But hey, Liz added sprinkles.

The contrast of their ice cream selection was just another example of how they couldn't be any more different.

Liz always took care to present herself a specific way—hair always styled and usually dressed in a dress or skirt and heels. Reflecting, I realized I'd never seen her in sneakers or with her hair tied back.

Reaching across the table, I brushed her hair over her shoulder. The lack of electricity was apparent. Flashbacks of Daisy touching my chest played. The spark, the fire, I felt there was nowhere to be found with the woman sitting across from me.

"What're you doing?" she blushed.

"I just realized I've never seen you with your hair back," I shrugged. "I was curious."

Pulling a hair tie from her small designer bag, she secured her hair in a low bun.

"What do you think?" she smiled, flirting.

"Nice," I smiled back. Her smile faltered a little, and guilt struck me. I knew what she wanted to hear, but I couldn't bring myself to compliment her anymore with a certain firecracker on my mind.

"Was that the girl from the pottery shop?" Caught off guard by her question, I nodded, unable to form words. "She's such a mess. I mean, I would never leave the house in my pajamas like that. She clearly has no respect for herself."

"At least she has respect for others," I snapped without thinking.

"Excuse me?"

"You were incredibly disrespectful the other night. How you treated Daisy was unacceptable. That's why I sent you home—I stayed behind to help her clean up. Something *you* should have done." She sat stunned, and I continued without thinking. "For the record, I like the way she dresses."

Abruptly, Liz got to her feet and put her hands on her hips. "You were supposed to be apologizing to me, not berating me."

Groaning, I rubbed my face. My eyes were covered, but I still felt her presence.

"Can we go, please?"

I looked up, unsure if I heard her correctly. "You want to go? With me?"

"Don't be silly," she scoffed. "Of course I want to go with you. I'm still upset, but I'm sure I can find a way for you to make it up to me." She eyed me suggestively and my stomach turned.

Depositing our leftovers in the trash, we walked back to my car. As we pulled onto Main Street, I felt a hand slide over my thigh. Using her nails, she trailed her hand further up my leg. But again, I felt nothing except annoyance. Thankfully, her hand traveled no further than a few inches above my knee.

The sound of the road beneath us was all that filled the space as I sat tense under her touch. The Dickover's family home came into view. The expansive colonial home sat on a lot an acre larger than my parents. A large ornate fountain decorated the middle of the courtyard, which was surrounded by a paved circular driveway. Perfectly trimmed and shaped trees lined the path to the front door.

Darkness took over the sky on our drive over. Meticulously selected lamp posts lit the front of the house as I walked Liz to the front door. At twenty-nine, Liz lived with her parents. There was nothing wrong with that part—I had friends at thirty-two living with their parents. The difference was they were saving, working towards a better future. Liz had no desire to do anything more than stay on-top of designer names and the latest scandal. I had the sneak suspicion she was waiting for the next person to take on the task of caring for her. Which really meant funding her lifestyle.

After high school, Liz tried college but was kicked out when the school figured out her scheme. She'd found a look-a-like to test her out of half her classes. She had the classic "money rules the world" mentality. Since then, she had kept busy with social clubs, but never bothered with a job.

Regardless of how I felt about Liz, I was still a gentleman, and I was still playing a part. By her side, I walked her to the front door.

"So…" her voice trailed as she looked up at me.

"I'm sorry for the way I spoke to you," I said, looking away and choking on the words.

"I forgive you," she slid her hands up my chest, clasping them behind my neck. She was forward with that she wanted, and I wasn't oblivious to it. But, at that moment, there was nothing I wanted less. Maybe because everything with Daisy was fresh, I felt this way. Maybe the lack of time passing was the only reason it felt so uncomfortable. Maybe it would get better.

Instead of retreating, I sighed and placed a light kiss on her lips.

She moaned, and I hated myself for thinking that it didn't compare to the music of Daisy's moan. Her lips parted, inviting me to take more. Maybe it would get better another day, but for the time being, my heart wasn't in it. Before she could take it further, I pulled away.

"Have a good night."

"Good night!" Liz called after excitedly as I walked down the stairs.

Hurriedly, I drove home, needing to take a shower to wash away the disgusting feeling the clashing emotions gave me. Under the stream of hot water, I gripped my erection and tugged. Daisy's name was on my lips as I reached completion for the fourth time since our kiss only the night before.

Thinking of my current situation—the boring and entitled brunette I didn't want and the freewheeling sunshine in human form I couldn't have—I rested my head against the cool tile.

What did I do?

fifteen

daisy

"You'll mainly be focused on register, bar and clean-up in your role until you're more comfortable with other tasks. How do you feel about learning about glazing and firing?" I asked the tall, bright-eyed woman. Polly's first day had gone off without a hitch and she got the hang of the register and layout quickly.

"I feel like that sounds like the coolest thing in the world," she said with a big grin, eagerly shaking her head in acceptance.

In recent recovery, Polly was eighty-two days sober and a total badass. Over lunch, my new hire treat, of course, she told me of her journey. Poppy, her seventeen-year-old daughter, inspired her to get sober. She'd just won a full-ride academic scholarship to Penn State. Pride made her want to be totally present for her high school graduation...and the rest of her life.

Being sober, she now also had the wherewithal to hold a steady job. They'd been getting by on her late husband's life insurance, but funds were running out quick. She needed additional income and wanted to send her daughter off to college with a hefty savings account.

With teary eyes, Polly thanked me for the opportunity, and with equally teary eyes, I gave her hand a squeeze. I rubbed at the ache in my chest as we nibbled on homemade chips and panini's. Through the pain of what I missed out on, hope bloomed at the thought that Polly's daughter would have the mother I never did.

The sharp ring of the phone interrupted our conversation.

"You wanna get it?" I asked Polly.

"I would love to," Polly cheerily skipped to the front desk. *Ah, new job bliss.* "Slay and Clay, this is Polly." Silently nodding, she looked at me expectantly. "Sure, one moment. It's for you." She said, covering the mouthpiece.

Taking her place on the phone, I answered. "Hello, this is Daisy." I held my breath, half expecting the voice of the person on the other side.

"She sounds pretty," Carl sadistically snarled. "Better warn her. I'm on my way to beat your ass, your mother's ass, and any other pretty little ass-"

I slammed the phone down with a suppressed scream. As to not scare my desperately needed new employee, I restrained myself from slamming the phone multiple times, as I'd become accustomed to every time I got off the phone with Carl.

My temple throbbed; with a sigh, I rubbed at the spot.

"All good, boss?" Polly asked sweetly, her eyes wide.

"Yes, yep. Great." Rubbing at the pulse on the side of my head, I drew a breath. "Listen, there's something I need to tell you. There is a man that has been calling and threatening me and the business. He's my mom's latest ex, and he's a nasty, awful, man with a big ego—dangerous combo. I'm working with the police to build a case for a protective order." I sighed and made a mental note to visit Kendrick this week at the station.

"Also, I need to figure out how the hell to block a number on a landline. In the meantime, just be aware, never close alone, and let me know if anything happens to make you feel unsafe or uncomfortable.

Also, write on a sticky note whenever he calls with the date and time, and message if you speak with him."

"Understood..." her voice trailed off. She wrung her hands and looked like she had more she wanted to say. Patiently, I waited for her to continue. "I have a contact at the woman's shelter," there was a tint of shame in her voice, and I understood the story that was unspoken. She'd had a rough last seven years, with her husband dying and her boyfriend being no better than Carl. "He can probably help with the phone issue. Or at least give us some tips on how to handle the situation."

"That's a great idea, Polly. Thank you for that offer, I'd love to meet him." With all sincerity, I rubbed her arms. "Thank you."

Her shy smile did something to my resolve. Between that and her vulnerability earlier, I felt compelled to tell her about Sandy.

"Since we're on the topic," I started quietly, "I have a few other things I wanted to share with you. My mother, Sandy, is an alcoholic. I've been trying to help her, but she's been resistant. It's a long story. Anyway, she recently stole three thousand dollars from me before fleeing. She hasn't been back since, but that's why her ex, Carl, keeps calling. I've tried to get her to visit a women's shelter, and seek help, but you probably know better than me..."

My voice shook as I spoke. No one knew the story, or the entirety of what I was going through, except for me. And now Polly. Not even Ellie. The truth was hard to speak aloud but was made easier by the kindness seeping from Polly.

"You have to admit you need help first." Polly softly finished my sentence.

Unable to speak, I gave a small nod. Polly took my hands into hers before continuing. "Thank you for sharing. I know it can't be easy.

If you're interested, the shelter also hosts an Al-Anon meeting once a week. It's for people dealing with a loved one's alcoholism."

"Yeah, maybe," I nodded. "That sounds good."

"Great, I'll get some info for you." Polly pulled me into a tight hug. "I think I'm going to love working here."

"Well, I can tell you I already love having you here, Pol."

sixteen

daisy

"HI-YA, GERALDINE. LOOKING LOVELY today," I greeted my regular pottery star with a big smile. Since that night at my shop where she stood up for me against Liz, she'd been at the top of my list of favorite people. "Green is your color, girl."

"Daisy!" she greeted me with enthusiasm. "What brings you here?"

"Just hoping to see Officer Lawson. Is he in?"

"He sure is," Geraldine looked over her shoulder slyly. "Looking mighty handsome today, if you ask me. Just walk straight back and his desk is on the left."

With thanks from me, and a wink from Geraldine, I walked between the rows of desks. The wooden tops and steel legs of each desk were identical. The desks sat in perfect order, as if someone copy and pasted the layout. Personal touches highlighted the differing personalities of every officer. Each was littered with pictures of families, empty cups of coffee, and sticky notes with names and numbers.

Cataloging each desk as I walked past, I took in the personal mementos and wondered what I would have at a desk.

On one sat a family photo—a boy in a cap and gown, a girl in a flowered dress. They made silly faces at the camera as a middle-aged woman kissed a stocky man's cheek. Immediately, I recognized the man to be Hugo. Every Thursday evening he'd walk into Loop &

Scoop, the ice cream parlor I worked at with Ellie many moons ago, with his wife on his arm and his children skipping ahead. I even remember their orders—More O'Smores for Hugo, because he had good taste, Raspberry Razzle for his wife, Pam, Turtle Truffle for the boy, and Cotton Candy for the girl.

On another desk, there were three empty coffee mugs. In the corner, next to the monitor, sat an ornate framed photo of a grumpy cat. Caffeine addiction and an abundantly loved angry looking cat meant that was Walt's desk.

In stark contrast was another desk, not a thing out of place. The only giveaway was the screensaver. Two motorcycles at the edge of a canyon. A jovial man occupied one muscle cycle, and a woman doing the iconic *rock on* sign with her pinky and pointer finger pointing skyward, occupied the other. Kelly was the town's resident badass, and everyone knew it. She and her husband, Abe, always led the memorial day parade through downtown, flying flags off the back of their seats.

Maybe my desk would have a picture of me and Ellie in our paper boat shaped hats. Maybe I'd make a little pen holder out of clay—shape it like a flower, or a bumblebee, or maybe an elephant, and I'd make it so it held pens in its trunk. Maybe that would be an alternate universe where I'd have more childhood photos than my one tattered one from a carnival when I was eleven. Maybe in that alternate universe, my stay in Chestnut Hills wasn't the longest I ever stayed somewhere. Maybe it was a universe where I would have friends from middle school, and family, and friends of family that I called aunt and uncle, as it seemed like everyone else in this town had.

The call of my name pulled from my daydream. Sat to the right was Kendrick, a big smile on his face; it sparkled against the dark of his skin and brought with it an adorable dimple of each side of his face.

"Officer," I greeted warmly.

"Hello," he said, his eyes raking me. "To what do I owe this gorgeous intrusion?"

Kendrick's desk was the most personable of all. A green leather desk pad laid beneath everything, and a very refined looking leather three-tier file organizer sat in the corner. One of those perpetual calendars stood next to the file organizer, but it was made unique designed as a vintage arcade game. His keyboard with the light up keys and mouse with the ergonomic slopes looked high end compared to the standard issue. A mini barbell set-up held his pens, which seemed funny next to a mini Zen Garden.

"You like to scrape sand and chill out after throwing weights around?" I joked as I approached.

"It's called balance, Bloom." His flourish of a wink was charming. There was no denying that. But disappointment bubbled when it didn't tickle my tummy the same way Reid did.

Promptly, I took a seat in the vinyl and plastic chair at the side of his desk. Crossing my ankles, I made myself comfortable before placing a stack of notes on his desk with a soft thud. Details from the call from earlier today sat on top.

"Seriously?" his flirtatious tone was gone and replaced with disbelief as his smile dropped.

Silently, he flipped through the small square pieces of paper. Skimming every detailed incident, I could see the crease between his brow deepen with each new page. Realization hit me and my stomach dropped.

My ugly past had caught up to me. But I didn't work from nothing, build a whole new life for myself from nothing, *for* nothing. No one was going to take that away from me, and especially not woman-hating-abusive-alcoholic-Carl. I wasn't going to run away, and I sure as hell wasn't going to roll over and take it.

I was in control.

"I was training the new gal, a woman named Polly, when he called to say he was on his way to beat me up. Carl is a lot of things, but a liar isn't one of them. As long as I've known him, when he made threats, he kept them." A flashback played of the day he told me he was going to put me in a coma. While I made it through, that doesn't change the fact that I almost didn't or that he made good on his words.

"Anyhow...that was a pretty potent reminder to come by and give you the latest update," I explained.

He nodded in understanding. Rummaging through the bottom drawer on his right, he pulled out a manila folder labeled *Daisy*. In it, he revealed a pile comprising every note I had given him. Looking down at the mixed pieces of paper, he lifted a sticky note I had left in his mailbox last week.

"I've been meaning to ask, where does one find sticky notes with dancing cartoon hot dogs?" he asked.

"The internet is a vast place," I quirked an eyebrow. "Just wait until you see the goldfish with the booties."

"Booties?" he was laughing now.

"Yep, big and juicy butts. Whoever drew them gave them big, pronounced peaches right above their tail fin. It's an abomination—and a total hit when anyone sees them."

"You are something else, Daisy Bloom." He gave me a long look; determined, I held his gaze. If a certain number crunching drummer who I will not name wanted nothing to do with me, there was a handsome, funny man who did. Taking a deep breath, he refocused his attention. "Well, I think we have more than enough here. I'll help you get the paperwork started and we can file with the court."

"Thanks Kendrick," I stood to make my leave. "You are a cliché of a hometown hero. Don't let it get to your head."

Halfway down the aisle, I turned as I his deep voice called my name.

"Have dinner with me," he commanded with a lightness to him. His smirk was panty melting. At least it would have been if it weren't for the pest that was Reid popping back into my head.

What the hell? I deserved to have a little fun. A girl could do a lot worse than Officer Kendrick Lawson.

With a wink, I turned on my heel, walking out. "You know where to find me."

seventeen

reid

"Reid, I love it when you grace our doorstep. Come on in." Elaine opened the door wide.

"Good morning, Mrs. Dickover," I greeted, stepping over the threshold. "Is Liz ready?"

Calling Liz's name up the grand swirling staircase, Elain returned to me with a smile.

"I'm so glad you two are finally giving things a chance," she said, eyeing me. "I've dreamed of this day since Liz first told me of her crush in seventh grade."

Though it was an innocent enough comment, it grated against my insides. I wondered if she knew about the extortion of it all.

"Seventh grade, huh?" I offered a small smile, doing my best to convey friendliness. It'd already been a month since the unforgettable kiss I shared with Daisy, and ever since then, I had been making a conscious effort to put it out of my mind. If that meant fully embracing my new *relationship*, then that was what I was going to do.

Liz came gingerly down the stairs. As always, she was in her signature style. Today, her dress was a little more on the casual side. The ironed sheath dress stopped just above her knee, adorned with big brass buttons on the side pockets and on the thick straps. Nestled in her brown hair, she had placed a headband in the same shade of white, matching the color of her short heels.

"Liz, not that you don't look lovely, but do you think that's the best outfit for a farmer's market?" I asked.

She paused halfway down the stairs and frowned. "You don't like it?"

"It's not that. I just want you to be comfortable on the gravel and grass in this heat."

A smile replaced the frown on her face. "You're so considerate." With a graceful descent down the remaining steps, she made her way to the front, where we met. Sweetly, she pressed a gentle kiss against my lips.

As she always did, apparently regardless of the audience, she tried coaxing my tongue into her mouth. While I hadn't yet yielded to the game of cat-and-mouse, it seemed inevitable that I would have to, eventually. Elaine stood only a foot away as I pulled away. With a cheerful expression, she had her hands clasped at her chest.

Laughing uncomfortably, I walked Liz to the front door and guided her into the car parked outside.

Chestnut Hills had a weekly farmer's market year round all day every Saturday. But from June to September, the first market of the month started on Friday night for First Fridays. Live music and food trucks accented the block party vibe. Crafts and small business vendors lined the street, bringing eclectic variety over the standard produce and meat vendors at the farmer's market.

Today, a local DJ, a student at the Chestnut Hills Community College, was on stage mixing pop hits and 90s hip hop. The music filtered through the large speakers littered up and down the road.

Holding Liz's hand, I helped stabilize her as she walked over the gravel of the parking lot. I couldn't help but think about how I should have tried harder to convince her to change shoes.

"Isn't this cute?" she asked, taking it in. A condescending tone laced her words, making my eye involuntarily twitch.

"Haven't you been here before?" I returned her question with my own, surprised. Everyone who had lived in town for the summer months had been to at least *one* First Fridays. That was the main reason the Assets never played one—I still tried to keep my drumming hidden from my family. Though, soon enough, I'm sure it would permeate my parents' social circles as we continued to gain popularity.

"Nope. It's always felt a little," she paused, searching for the word, "kitschy."

I held my eyes from rolling and instead pulled my hand from hers and placed it in my pocket. Being with Liz wasn't the worst thing ever, but when she said shit like that, it made my blood boil. How easy it was for her to act so above other people was unsettling.

Instead of taking the hint at my discomfort, she looped her arm around mine. Thankful that the path was a mix of pavement and grass, I didn't have to worry about keeping her steady. The row of tables that lined both sides were colorful and exciting. The talent showcased by each artist was impressive.

The call of my name caught my attention. Looking over my shoulder, I caught Ellie and Theo walking towards me, hand in hand.

"Reid," Ellie greeted cheerfully, pulling me into a hug.

"Hey guys," I said, shaking Theo's hand. Ellie cut me off before I could introduce the couple.

"Sometimes I sing with..." her voice trailed off as she caught my wide eyes and slight shake of my head. "With...myself. Yeah, no one likes to hear me sing more than myself."

She laughed nervously as Theo pulled her in. "That's not true. I love to hear you sing."

Watching their lovesick stares, Liz nudged my side and introduced herself. "I'm Liz, Reid's girlfriend."

A flash of surprise quickly appeared and disappeared from their faces before Ellie and Theo both greeted her warmly. I couldn't help but ruminate on why they would be surprised. Was this farce so unbelievable that the first reaction to our relationship was surprise?

Another couple came up behind the pair, and Theo introduced them as his sister, Thalia, and her husband, Marc. Our conversation was interrupted when Thalia let out a shriek.

"Omg, that booth has hand carved baby mobiles." She slapped her husband's chest. Turning back to us, she explained, "I'm pregnant. It's still early, but the nesting bug has bitten me."

Giving our congratulations, Liz surprised me by offering to walk over with Thalia to scope out the nursery décor. With a larger-than-life grin, Thalia gladly accepted. Rising to her tiptoes, Liz brushed a kiss on my cheek before walking over with Thalia.

"So, Liz." Ellie said as more of a statement than anything.

Rocking on my heels, I wondered what Daisy had told her. "Yep. Liz."

"Interesting…"

Assessing each other, we both narrowed our eyes, trying to read each other's minds.

"Marc," Theo interrupted, "why don't we go pick out some flowers for Mom? That stand has hydrangeas." Taking the bait, the two walked away in the other direction.

"Hey, I don't judge your partner choices." I said to Ellie as soon as we were alone.

"Not judging, just curious." She held up her hands in surrender. "She doesn't seem your type."

My jaw ticked at being clocked so easily. "Tell me, what is my type?"

"Well, I'm not sure, to be honest. But I can think of a certain blonde, whom I swear I saw sparks between you two." I said nothing, and she continued to assess me. "I saw you two fighting a month ago, and I thought maybe there was something there."

Ellie shrugged, and I realized Daisy hadn't told her friend anything. Decidedly, I kept my mouth shut.

"But then she started dating Kendrick, and I thought maybe I was wrong. But now, seeing you with Liz, I'm thinking I wasn't and you're both running from something. But that's just my uneducated best friend intuition taking a guess."

"Daisy and Kendrick?" my brows hit my hairline with surprise, and I felt like I'd been punched in the gut.

Ignoring my question, she continued. "Also, does she not know you drum? That's like half your personality." She threw her hands up in exasperation.

"Daisy and Kendrick?" I asked again.

"Yep, the cute cop," she eyed me suspiciously, then dropped her jaw in realization. "I knew there was something going on with you two."

"There is nothing going on between me and Daisy."

"Uh huh, tell that to your face."

Before I could ask more questions about Kendrick, the men returned with several bouquets at the same time Thalia and Liz returned empty-handed.

"We are so ordering from them in a few months," Thalia said, handing her husband a business card.

Taking the card, Marc handed her a small bouquet of freshly cut farm flowers. "I'll trade you, gorgeous."

"And for you, my love," Theo brandished a similar bouquet from behind his back, giving them to Ellie.

As Liz and I watched them exchange kisses and *I love you*s, she leaned into me. "I want flowers," she whispered.

Walking away with her own bouquet of flowers, Liz looped her arm in mine again. Ellie's accusations replayed in my head. If I was going to live on like this, convince everyone around me this was what I wanted, I had to try harder. Taking the bouquet from her, I laced the fingers of my other hand with hers.

Nearing the end of the booths, a vibrantly decorated tent caught my eye. A bright pink and yellow banner read *Slay & Clay*. My stride paused, and my eyes searched for her, just for a moment.

A head of blonde caught my eye, pink strands sticking out. My heart began beating faster as I took in her wild hair, frizzy from the heat. She was wearing a fringe strapless top in electric blue, and though I couldn't see her bottom half, I imagined she paired it with a flowy white skirt, or patterned shorts. When it came to her, nothing was off the table.

My throat constricted as I watched a dark-skinned man with a crisp fade lean in to kiss her cheek. His deep blue uniform gave it away, and I knew it was Kendrick.

Before I could steer us away, Liz was dragging me towards the table.

"I think I want a new vase for my flowers," she said cheerily.

Daisy's wide eyes knocked the breath out of me. The vast ocean her eyes held called me in like a sailor to the sea. It took a moment, but I finally managed a wave.

"Hey man," Kendrick greeted. Regretfully, I shook his outstretched hand.

"Hey," I replied, trying to avoid Daisy's burning stare.

Kendrick looked between me and Daisy. "Aren't you going to say hi to my girl?" he asked, putting his arm around her and pulling her in.

Hurt bubbled in my chest as he said *my girl*. "Hey Daisy," I offered with a small smile. With a smile mirroring mine, she redirected her attention to Liz.

"So, what'cha looking for?" Daisy asked cheerfully. Knowing her, though, she was probably cursing Liz for her treatment at the Paint and Sip night. And she was probably cursing me for, well, for everything.

"A vase," Liz territorially pulled me to her. "My handsome boyfriend surprised me with flowers, and I need a new vase to match."

If by surprise she meant she picked out the flowers she explicitly asked for, then sure, I surprised her. I began inching away, trying to remove myself from her grasp. Daisy drew Liz away, showing her the display of vases. Kendrick and I stood, looking on.

"You good?" he asked.

"Great."

"You sure? You look a little green, and I feel like I sensed something weird between you two. I'm not encroaching on something, am I?"

I looked at Liz and reminded myself of my choices. Of whom my girlfriend was.

"Nah man," I cleared my throat. "Liz and I are dating now. I haven't spoken to Daisy in a few weeks, so it was a surprise to see her here." It pained me to speak the words. This was the second time in the last hour I had to lie about my history with Daisy. "So, you two, huh?" I asked my old friend. We weren't as close as we used to be, but the friendship was easy to fall back into.

"Yep, she's pretty awesome. A little closed off, but a total firecracker."

I nodded in understanding because of just that. I understood. Better than anyone knew.

Liz picked a soft pink vase that featured bubbly hearts popping up all around. It wasn't something she would typically go for. Immediately, I knew it was all Daisy's influence. I cursed, knowing I was going to have to look at that vase for God knew how long and be reminded of the one who got away every time.

Handing my debit card over, Daisy pushed it away.

"On the house." She refused to look at me as she packaged the vase. First wrapping it in tie-dye tissue paper, she stuffed it in a lime green paper bag.

"I can't accept that. Please," I pushed the card back towards her.

She gave us a smile, but I read the anger in her eyes. Her words sounded genuine to the untrained ear, but I caught the disdain they dripped with.

"For the happy new couple."

eighteen
daisy

"WHERE'S YOUR HEAD?" KENDRICK asked from across the table.

It was our seventh date, and it had been perfect. Aside from the barrage of intrusive thoughts about a particularly grumpy man named Reid, I'd been happy to spend this time with Kendrick.

Brass sconces hung on the walls every six feet. Those and the candles at the center of each table were the only sources of light. The light, though dim, enveloped us in warmth. Oil paintings and mirrors with ornate frames covered the brick walls, which went perfectly with the lace linen covering each table. Nestled in the basement of an old church, the ambiance was hypotonic.

Textbooks would define the evening as a perfect, romantic night. Kendrick picked me up with a beautiful bouquet of wildflowers, an array of colors poking out in every direction. On the drive to the city, he'd kept the conversation going and played with my hair as if it was an everyday occurrence.

Until that point, we'd kissed only a few times. At first, my body would awaken at the sensation of kissing, but then quickly shut down. Let it be known, it had absolutely nothing to do with the kissing partner. Let me tell you—that man was talented. Any other woman would have swooned, melted into a puddle, or proposed on the spot. Not me though. Nope. A good, kind, genuine man comes into my life and I can't get past first base because he wasn't the one guy I couldn't get out of my head.

How much longer could I have kept it going, though? Kenrick deserved to find someone who could meet his affection with enthusiasm. He didn't deserve to be with someone who didn't return his interest tenfold.

That's where my head was—involuntarily focused on the tall, dark-haired, forearm flexing, head banging sexy man. Since seeing him with the woman who purposely spilled wine at a pottery paint night, his presence in my mind had doubled. I accepted his decision, but I knew I couldn't keep pretending it didn't affect me.

Especially not if it meant stringing the man sitting across from me along.

Looking Kendrick in his deep, chocolaty brown eyes, I gave him a small smile.

"I'm sorry, Kenny," the use of my affectionate nickname for him was a ploy in the hopes of softening the blow. "I can't be fully present with you. My focus has been somewhere else, and that isn't fair to you."

"I see," he nodded, taking a sip of his water. "This wouldn't happen to do with Reid by chance, would it?"

Stunned, my mouth hung open. "I-I don't know...maybe." Frustration I hadn't acknowledged yet bubbled to the surface.

"Hey, it's okay," he reached his hand across the table, giving my hand a squeeze. "I appreciate the honesty. And if we're being real, I half expected it. You two were making heart eyes that day at the shop, after the break-in. Then at the fair he looked like a wounded puppy."

Feeling inappropriately smug, I smiled to myself at Kendrick's observation. Probably not the time or place for that feeling.

Kendrick chuckled. "And, let's just say he should be thankful you don't harness the power of lasers for eyes. He would've been fried on the spot."

I laughed at the picture he painted, and at the truth of it.

"I know you just ended things with me and all, but I'd love for us to stay for dessert. I wouldn't forgive myself if I went home single *and* banana pudding-less."

"You're too good of a man, Kenny."

nineteen

daisy

"Pocket Full of Sunshine" reverberated through Bertha's speakers. The sun was high and bright as I drove along the main road out of downtown. Windows down, I let my hair freely swirl around me. Embracing the free feeling driving with the windows down gave me, I sang loudly along with the music.

It'd been two weeks since my dinner with Kendrick. In that time I had yoga'd all the yoga and Om'd all the Om's in a futile attempt to release my anger with Reid.

Reid had let me down—big time. Not that he'd know it, but it was rare for me to open up, and even rarer for me to consider anything more serious than a short-term fling.

Kendrick was a catch of a human, not someone you "fling" with. If I couldn't be with Reid, and if I wanted to consider the possibility of letting myself be locked down by a man, Kendrick would've been the guy. But Reid went and ruined that for me with his perfect fucking face and his stupid considerate nature and his dumb talents like being academic *and* creative.

This whole thing also made me realize I had a thing for forearms. That was almost more enraging than knowing he was with the "don't you live on tips?" girl.

Relationships weren't even a thing I did, and this was exactly why. Feelings, dependencies, self-doubt. And if there was one thing about me, it was that self-doubt was nowhere in my repertoire. Except, recently, it had been.

Natasha Bedingfield somehow made it all feel okay.

The song ended just as I pulled into the parking lot of Ellie's apartment complex. Locking the door behind me, I skipped along to the front door, eyeing the empty moving truck. The empty moving truck meant there was likely a bunch of stuff that still had to be packed up, and that meant I was in for a long day.

Ellie's apartment was in shambles. Trinkets and clothes littered every surface. I called my best friend's name, and she waltzed out of her room, flushed, with Theo right on her heels.

"Wow, we have work to do here, folks. Keep it in your pants for a few hours, okay?" I joked with exasperation.

"Good morning to you too, cranky pants," Ellie greeted, while Theo gave her a smack on the butt and disappeared into his apartment across the hall.

Pulling her into a hug, I gave her a big kiss on the cheek.

"My little Elle's, I'm so proud of you." I may have been teasing, but the tears in my eyes were real. Theo and her were inevitable, but I didn't think they'd move in together so quickly. Yet, with all the memories this place held for both of them, it made sense. They made sense.

My chest squeezed a little tighter with the love I felt for her...and was that longing? *Ew. No, Daisy. You don't want this; you want freedom and independence.*

"I love you, Daze."

"I love you, too."

"Okay, that's enough," Ellie laughed, wiping at her eyes. "Much to pack, little time."

Following Ellie into the room, I listened diligently as she directed me to finish cleaning out her closet.

While stuffing her dresses into bags, I overheard the unmistakable booming voice of Jake and the sweet sing-songy voice of Penny arrive to help. Jake took off to Theo's apartment as his voice disappeared.

Penny's floating head popped into the closet from behind the doorjamb. "Hi-ya, Daze."

"Penny!" Abandoning my duties for a split second, a gave Penny a breath-taking hug. "Alright, not to be rude, but we have a lot of shit to pack up. Lil ol' miss is somewhat of a hoarder, apparently."

"Clearly," Penny rang, picking up a lace peplum top. "Um, the 2010s called. They want their top back."

With a barking laugh, I snatched the shirt from her and packed it away. "That's what I said! But when you look like Ellie, I guess you can wear whatever you want."

Sending her on her way, I kept moving. The hoarder bit was a joke, but there really was a shitload of stuff to pack. Digging through her stack of folded shirts, my hand grazed a hidden object. Was it...? No, not sweet Ellie. It couldn't be.

Placing the shirts in their assigned cardboard box, while maintaining their perfect folds, I turned to find a goldmine and screamed in surprise. Grabbing the item and rushing into the living room, I screeched.

"Ellie, you closet freak!" I teased, holding a long whip. Playfully cracking it in the air, Ellie rushed over to grab it from me. Too quick for her, I gave her a good whack on the ass first.

"Hey, that's reserved for me," Theo joked, having ran in at my yelling.

"Nice," Jake laughed as he emerged behind Theo. He and Penny had followed in just in time to see the scene unfold and Penny slapped her fiancé's arm.

Embarrassed, Ellie hid the whip behind her back while side stepping behind a stack of boxes. She tried and failed to covertly hide the sex toy in a box labeled *BOOKS*.

"No need to be shy, dear. You should see the collection Pat and I have." Mrs. Hudson, Ellie's elderly neighbor who joined in on the packing, giggled. *You go, girl.* She'd been instrumental in Ellie and Theo's relationship and became a bit of a staple in our lives. A welcome one at that, with her slap-ya-across-the-face honesty and fruit salads.

Ellie turned beet red as her jaw hit the floor at the sweet old woman's confession. Theo laughed loudly, causing us all to fall into hysterics.

"Whoa, it's a party in here," a new voice tittered. It was the same voice that had haunted my dreams. Okay, maybe not that dramatic, but close. It was the same voice I'd dreamed of calling my name, the same voice I'd dreamed of surrendering to.

I froze, unsure of what to do with myself.

"What is Reid doing here?" I asked out of the side of my mouth, poking Ellie's side.

"What the hell is going on with you two?" throwing her hands in the air, Ellie was clearly annoyed and so over our shenanigans. She'd suspected us for a while, and I'd been expertly dodging her questioning. I only hadn't confided in her yet because I wasn't sure what there was to confide. Guilt consumed me and I looked away shyly.

"Nothing," we said in unison, too quickly.

"We're moving two apartments into one across town. We needed all the help we could get." Theo explained. The look of pride on his face was adorable and nauseating.

Reid's cool gray eyes met mine, and just as we did at the farmer's market a month ago, had a silent conversation. His end was full of pleading, begging for forgiveness. My end was just me silently giving him the middle finger.

"Thanks for helping Reid." Ellie walked over to him, wrapping him in an embrace. "Since you're here, I'm thinking the guys can start loading up the truck with the furniture while the gal's finish packing the boxes?"

"You got it, babe. Marc and Thalia will be here soon too," Theo gave Ellie a parting kiss on the temple, and the men disappeared with him.

As I packed the silverware into a small box cushioned with crumpled paper, I pretended not to notice as Reid lifted the coffee table. With a grunt that I'd only heard in my dreams, he hefted the small wooden table above his head. A tight grip on the edge kept it securely in place and the veins in his wrists, forearms, and neck tensed.

I scolded my panties. *Stay on, dammit.*

Mrs. Hudson left to make dinner for her husband; Marc and Thalia had to leave early for an appointment with a potential night nanny; and Jake and Penny had dinner with one of their future in-laws.

Ellie, Theo, Reid and I stared at the packed moving truck, each of us mirroring the other with our hands on our hips. Theo forcefully closed the rolling door, causing a loud clang to reverberate.

"Shit," Ellie exclaimed. "I forgot to grab the gardening supplies out of the storage unit." The end of her sentence turned into a whine. "I'm so tried...babe, can you get them for me?"

"Gardening supplies?" I asked. "You live in an apartment, and you're moving into another apartment. What the hell are you doing with gardening supplies?"

"They were a gift from Patty!" Ellie explained, referencing Theo's green-thumbed mom.

Rolling my eyes skyward, I took a deep breath. "Consider this your housewarming gift, because I forgot to stop by the store on the way here. I will get them for you."

"I love you, I love you, I love you," Ellie shrieked and promptly sat her butt on the curb.

Deep blues and purples painted the sky as we had worked straight through the day and evening, the night beginning to take over. I walked across the large parking lot to Ellie's still opened storage unit.

"I'll help," Reid called from behind me, his footsteps fast approaching.

"Goody," I said with the appropriate amount of sarcasm.

"Or I could let you carry all the tools by yourself and watch you struggle," he shot back.

"Or you could gracefully bow out of my life. What are you even doing here?"

"Helping Ellie move."

"But why? I thought you guys weren't that close."

"I overheard her telling Brian how stressed she was. It's his and his wife's anniversary tonight. He couldn't help, so I volunteered."

"Wow, how chivalrous." Stumbling into the dark unit, I turned on the flashlight setting of my phone. In the corner sat several large gardening tools, a hoe, a rake, a shovel, a fork, and some weird grabby cylinder thing. In a pile at the feet of the tools, smaller handheld versions were scattered about.

"What the hell is this?" I held up the unknown grabby cylinder thing, inspecting it.

"Pretty sure that's a posthole digger."

"What in the..." I trailed off, bewildered at my best friend. "Hey, I can do that myself," I begrudgingly said as I watched Reid put all the handheld tools into the empty canvas tote that laid next to them. With quick work, he gathered all the large tools into his arms while the tote hung from his wrist.

"I know you can," he grunted as he walked past, his arms full while I held the posthole digger. "I'm just not going to let you."

"Oh, so now you want to be considerate."

Ducking, I barely missed being decapitated by the shovel hanging over his shoulder as he whipped around.

"I was considerate. I stopped you before things went any further."

"Considerate would have been telling me during one of the countless times we hung out that you were engaged." Venom and disbelief made its way into my words. With a deep breath, I recalled all the Om's I had om'd and willed myself to calm.

"I'm not engaged!" he shouted now, taking a large step towards me. His scent invaded my space and his eyes grew wild.

"Considerate would have been not looking at me like that," I said firmly, doubling down.

His nostrils flared, "like what?"

"Like that," I looked between his eyes and my tone softened, "like how you're looking at me right now."

Our breaths quickened in sync, and I swear he drew his face closer. I could feel his breath coming in rough spurts. The wind picked up and the melodic tune of various wind chimes carried through the air. In the dark of the impending night, we were only illuminated by the moon and far away streetlamps.

"You guys need..." Theo's voice drew us out of our trance, "...help? Sorry, I didn't mean to interrupt."

My eyes remained locked on Reid's. Without a second look, I stepped around him and walked past Theo towards the truck. "You didn't interrupt anything."

twenty

reid

WAITING FOR MY EGG to reach perfect doneness, I yawned. Helping Ellie and Theo move depleted me physically. Seeing Daisy depleted me emotionally. Sleep evaded me as I tossed and turned all night.

Initially, I did offer to help because Ellie was visibly stressed with the move. With Brian being out of town, they'd be down a pair of hands, and I was more than happy to help a friend. Then, when I realized Daisy would likely be there, I was more motivated to show up. Even more motivated so than when I learned how to bake so I could ask my high school crush to prom with a homemade cake.

Given how my prom-posal didn't exactly pan out, you'd think I'd learn better than to have any sort of expectations. The Monday I showed up with my chocolate frosted goodness, my crush was gone. Just as such, the evening turned sour when I saw the disdain in Daisy's eyes as she looked at me.

I couldn't be swayed, though. I needed a glimpse of her. I needed to hear her laugh. I needed to confirm for myself that I'd made the right decision. Two halves of my heart fought a battle of two loves—my family and the blonde, feisty and energetic woman who had set my life on fire.

Replaying the conversation outside of the storage unit only riled my frustration more. Every day that passed by, I struggled more and more with my decision.

Gruffly, I sat myself at the small breakfast table in the corner of the tight kitchen with my fresh cup of coffee and plated eggs, toast, and sliced tomato. Focused on myself, I didn't hear Chuckie enter the kitchen and pour himself cereal until he spoke.

"You good, man?" he asked, pulling me from my thoughts. His hair stuck out in every direction, unbrushed since rolling out of bed. It worked with the hole in the collar of his shirt to paint a picture of Sunday laziness.

Looking up in confusion, he nodded to my plate. "You're about to cut through that plate with a spoon—also, you're eating a fried egg with spoon."

I cursed, throwing the spoon down.

"Chill, dude. What'd the spoon do to you?" Chuckie asked, scratching at his chest.

Until this point, Chuckie and I had barely had any conversation aside from anything about bills, who would get the last yogurt, and the latest episode of Bake-Off.

I thought about how he had zero connection to my family or my friends and thought, *fuck it*. Between sips of coffee, I unloaded my troubles.

"Damn," he said, sitting back and pushing his hand through his hair.

"Exactly," I agreed. "I just don't know what to do. Do I stick with my decision and be there for my family? Make the right choice? Or do what I want for myself?"

"You just said you think making the choice for your family is the right choice...but, I don't know, man. What makes that the right choice?"

I contemplated it, unsure how to even answer. "Family. We're supposed to do things for family, right?"

"Sure, but not things that make you miserable. And when you talk about this Liz chick, you sound fucking miserable, dude."

I didn't respond because he was right. Distracted with the thought, I spun my mug around in circles against the tabletop.

"I had this Great Uncle Ernie. Everyone thought he was gonna be a doctor or some shit. My great grandparents, all his siblings. So, all his life, they all acted like that was gospel. Lil' Ernie was gonna be a doctor. Well, one month into his residency, he disappeared. *Poof.* Left some note about how being a doctor was never his passion, and he needed time to figure out what his real passion was.

"Three years later, he mails my family a newspaper clipping that he won first place in a fishing competition. Apparently, he made a life fishing in the Everglades for a living. He came back to retire and be near family, and I tell you what—he said his only regret was not quitting school sooner.

"I don't know much, man, but I know if you make a decision like this for someone else, you'll never be happy." Silence hung as I contemplated his words and wondered why we hadn't had conversations like this sooner.

He sighed before standing. "Anyway, I hope you figure it out. I gotta go pick my girlfriend up from the airport."

"You have a girlfriend?" I asked, feeling guilty. How had we lived together, and I didn't even know he had a girlfriend?

"Yep, two years and counting. She's finally moving here from Florida. Shit," he scratched at his head. "By the way, you care if she stays here for a while until we find a new place?"

"All good," I laughed. For being so nonchalant about his day-to-day, Chuckie sure gave good advice. "Thanks for your help. It's given me a lot to think about."

Sighing, I realized what I had to do. Dialing on my phone, I was greeted as the ringing line was picked up. "Hey, are you free for lunch?" I asked, a lump clogging my throat.

Liz had her napkin laid gracefully across her lap. Her right shoe, a short but sensible heel with a gold designer emblem, dangled from her foot as her leg perched over her left knee. Despite me knowing her particular nature and uptightness, she presented herself as a picture of ease and comfort.

"Would it kill her to put on a little lipstick?" she asked in a conspiratorial, hushed tone.

Looking around, it took me a moment to realize she was criticizing the waitress. The eager and young college aged girl had been nothing but kind and helpful. Between chatting with us about the nice weather, complimenting Liz's dress, and rattling off the day's specials, I'm not sure where Liz found the time to nitpick at her appearance. Groaning, I took a sip of my water.

"I won't be joining in on whatever you're talking about."

She took her turn to groan, looking skyward. Sat outside at a small café table, we took in the sun's warmth and the sounds of families enjoying the Sunday evening. "You always act like you're so much better than me," she whined. Ice clinked in her glass as she fidgeted with her straw.

The comment caught me off-guard, and I couldn't hide my surprise. "What?"

"You always act like you're so much better than me," she repeated. "'I won't be joining in on that,' 'don't say that,' 'why do you do that?'" she deepened her voice in a poor imitation of me.

Processing the sheer balls on this woman, I bit my tongue. That I'm aware of how I treat and speak about people comes off to her as thinking I'm better than her, says it all. I wanted to tell her she was the most pretentious, judgmental person I'd ever met. I wanted to rehash every instance she was referring to and explain exactly how she'd behaved inappropriately or meanly. Instead, I took a big gulp of my iced tea.

"We should see other people," I stated flatly, wanting to get it over with.

Having just taken a bite of bread, it fell out of her mouth, half-chewed. Her jaw hung slack. "Wh-what?" she stuttered.

"We should see other people," I repeated. "We clearly have deep differences. I don't see this going anywhere."

"I see it going somewhere!" her voice reached new heights as she began screeching.

"Where? A loveless marriage and divorce court?" I immediately regretted my tone and tried to take it back. "I'm sorry, that was uncalled for. Look, Liz, this just isn't working. Can you honestly look me in the eye and tell me you think we're compatible?"

Looking everywhere but at me, her eyes darted around. I sighed with resignation.

"Everyone deserves the love they want. The life they want. And we are not what the other wants. You want someone to gossip with and pay for your shopping sprees. I want..." I trailed off, not finishing my sentence.

What did I want? Three months ago I would have said I wanted my freedom and control of my life. I would have said I wanted to be free of expectations or criticism from my parents. To be content. Those all sounded just as great now, but I couldn't help the longing in my chest that called to Daisy. Somehow, I felt that having Daisy would inevitably bring all those other things into fruition for me. She brought a lightness to me, to everything, and I craved it, needed it.

"What?" she asked, her sadness laced with questioning. "What do you want?"

I shook my head, clearing my thoughts. "I'm still figuring out what I want, but I know it's not this."

Nodding, she stood. Smoothing her dress with her palms, she brought her impossibly small designer bag up on her shoulder.

"Very well," she gave me a small smile, turning away. Not giving me a second glance, she walked to her Mercedes convertible her dad bought her for her twenty-eighth birthday and sped away.

The pavement moved under my feet in a blur. My rhythmic breathing accented my methodical stride as I ran towards downtown. The pond echoed the sounds of frogs, and the lambs at the farm across the way seemed to have grown. No geese today, I noted. Thank goodness for that.

The last week had been filled with self-reflection and band practice. With the weight of Liz gone, I'd slowly gotten my rhythm back. It wasn't as hard to get out of bed in the morning. Drumming was electrifying again. I was looking forward to our gig at Streets 7 last night. That was until I realized that with Ellie visiting her parents in Idaho with Theo, Daisy would be nowhere to be seen.

Disappointment clutched at my chest. The self-reflection I had been doing the week prior became clearer. I wanted Daisy. I knew she wanted me. But I had some things to make-up for, and I had to become the kind of man Daisy Bloom deserved.

Jogging the quiet streets of the town before the early birds and church goers began their mornings, I focused on only my breath and the timing of my stride. My stomach dropped as a familiar sight came into view. The roughest wave of déjà vu washed over me.

Red and blue flashed, reflecting off the shop windows. The silence of the street that was usually peaceful at this hour was now eerie with the emergency lights. My pace quickened as I ran towards the pottery studio. Coming upon the store front, my shoes crunched against the asphalt. Dread filled me as I noticed the darkened studio was exposed, the shop window now gone. In its place was an enormous gaping hole framed by jagged shards. Shattered glass littered the sidewalk. Taking in the scene, I quietly swore.

Tentatively entering, I looked around, assessing the scene. Broken pottery covered nearly every surface. It seemed as if there wasn't one piece intact. Tables and chairs were flipped. Paints and glazes were sprayed everywhere. A few of the built-in shelves had been broken into splinters, as if someone took a sledgehammer to them.

Sitting on the back staircase was Daisy, her face a mixture of anger and devastation. Hugging herself, her arms were crossed tightly. Kendrick and Kelly, another officer, stood in front of her; it looked as if they were speaking to her, but she wasn't present enough to comprehend.

I watched as her gaze landed on me. Life was breathed back into her in the form of exasperation and exhaustion. Uncrossing her arms, she clasped her hands, dropping them between her knees. Straightening, she rolled her eyes so hard I'd thought they would fall out. At least now I knew she was safe, and that fire still burned inside her. Relief washed over me at that and I released a breath I didn't realize I had been holding.

Kendrick and Kelly turned to see what caused her change in demeanor. After exchanging words, Kendrick walked towards me as Kelly redirected Daisy's attention elsewhere.

"Dude, what the hell happened?" I asked in a hushed tone, motioning around.

"Someone roughed up the place good. We're thinking it was probably the mom's jaded ex-boyfriend."

"Carl?" I snarled, aware of the stalking and threats. "How the hell did it get to this point?" The brief moment of relief has passed, and my anger and unease came creeping back.

"Listen, man, I'm just as frustrated as you. We've been working the law the best we can, but you can't control other people's actions."

"Aren't you guys seeing each other?" I shot back, my words laced with poison. "Shouldn't you have been here or at least helped her put up a better security system?"

"Don't be a dick, Reid. She has a state-of-the-art system; had it installed a few weeks ago when he told her he was on his way to come beat her up." Hearing the threat against her safety made my blood boil. I was worried that if I became any angrier, I'd combust. I hadn't known it'd gotten that far.

Looking back over his shoulder, he turned to me again, sighing heavily. "And we're not seeing each other. She dumped my fine uniformed ass for your stupid hot-headed ass."

This was news to me. "When?" My heart rate jumped, a lump forming in my throat. *There was a chance.*

"Like a month ago. Did you not know?"

My mind reeled as I tried processing the information. If they had broken up a month ago, that would mean she had broken things off before we saw each other at Ellie and Theo's. Our interactions replayed in my head, her anger at my presence. She had been so mad at me that night. Could it be because she was dealing with her feelings on top of ending things with Kendrick, Chestnut Hill's most eligible bachelor?

Shaking my head, I cleared those thoughts.

"Well, what is she going to do now?" I asked, changing the subject. "She can't stay here."

"I agree, but she refuses to leave. Something about not being able to leave her business."

Of course Daisy would refuse to leave. It being her business probably only had to do with it a little. Knowing her, it was more likely she wouldn't back down. Thanking Kendrick for sharing with me, I brushed past him.

Daisy was alone now. Catatonic, she was frozen, her eyes fixed forward. "Hey," my words were barely above a whisper, doing my best to soften my tone.

Meeting my gaze, I took in the wide-eyed look on her face. Her show of vulnerability wasn't something I'd ever seen, nor something I'd thought I'd ever see from her.

"Please save whatever smart-ass commentary you have. I'm kind of dealing with something here."

"No smart-ass commentary, promise." Sitting next to her on the step, I held up two fingers in a mock scout's honor. "I'm worried about you. How do you feel?"

"I feel sad, angry, embarrassed..." she wiped at a stray tear. "I feel like I'm at the mercy of someone else. I feel alone."

A sharp pain pierced my heart as her voice trailed off until it disappeared. My first instinct was to wrap her in warmth and sweet words. Instead, I laid a hand on her back and rubbed small circles.

"Where's skirt suit pre-Madonna?" she sniffled.

I laughed at the spot-on nickname. "At home with her parents, I assume. We broke up last week."

"My deepest condolences," she deadpanned, causing me to chortle. At least her sense of humor was still intact.

Lost in rubbing circles on her back, we sat in silence. I listened as her breathing steadied; I felt her muscles relax under my touch. There was no concept of time when it was just the two of us.

The police had left, heavy with the load of all the information Daisy could give them. More detailed accounts of Carl's calls, and copies of her security camera footage. The wreckage surrounded us as we continued to sit, unmoved.

Swallowing, I stood. Placing a kiss on the top of her head, I didn't dwell on how right the simple action felt.

"I'll be right back."

twenty-one
daisy

STEADYING MYSELF, I CLOSED my eyes and breathed rhythmically.

In through my nose, out through my mouth. In through my nose, out through my mouth.

My shop had been violated. My space had been violated. *I* had been violated. Fear still made me tremble as I thought back to the sound of the glass shattering. When alarm pings on my phone pulled me from my sleep, I became paralyzed.

The anger that seeped from the figure dressed in all black as it slammed into my built-in was palpable through the camera feed. I had never been more thankful for the overpriced, overcomplicated security system. Which now I was convinced was underpriced and perfectly complicated.

When the alert came through from the security company that they had alerted the police on my behalf, the sob I'd been holding back finally spilled free. I allowed myself to cry and shake until I heard the sirens near. By that time, the figure had disappeared.

Carl, as stupid as he was, had the wherewithal to cover his identity. The only mistake was he dropped his sledgehammer before he fled, hearing the sirens approaching. Hopefully it was enough for Kendrick and Kelly to trace back to him. Finally get that monster put away.

If my mom wasn't going to press charges for the horrible things he did to her—and me—then I would. By myself. Because I was alone.

Alone.

I was used to being alone. That was nothing new. Being alone didn't scare me; I always figured things out for myself. And, if for some ungodly reason, I couldn't figure it out, I'd make it up. Easy, peasy.

My eyes shot open at the sound of glass crunching, at the same time I jumped out of my skin.

"Sorry," Reid winced, returning.

His toned thighs peeked through the bottom of his running shorts. His black hair was tousled and frayed in every direction, as if he was just as stressed himself. His beard was perfectly trimmed and the brightness in his eyes was contrasted by the deepness of his worry lines.

His biceps flexed as they carried a tray of iced coffees and a box of treats from Meryl's Makes & Cakes. Setting the coffee and pastries in the spot he'd vacated next to me on the steps, he took a cup out of the carrier and placed in it my hand. Silently, he untied the pink ribbon and revealed a chocolate éclair that he placed in my other hand.

Blinking up at him, he looked at me pointedly. "Eat." The firmness in his voice, the command of it all, sent a tingle down my spine. If I wasn't dealing with the catastrophe that was my shop, I would've been inclined to reply *yes, daddy.*

I stared after him in awe as he piled the large pieces of debris near the front door. Satisfied with his first pass of the wreckage, he confidently stalked towards the supply closet. His frame filled the doorway, and then some, as I heard the clanging of whatever was last stuffed in there. Between me, Liam, and Calley, it was a toss up. Though Polly had been trying to recognize for us after binging "The Home Edit."

Emerging with a broom clutched tightly in his hand, he silently began sweeping the shattered glass and pottery into neat piles. With silent efficiency, he danced around, methodically sweeping.

The relief of having help washed over me in a way I wasn't prepared for. My shoulders loosened, and I did a few neck and shoulder rolls. Suddenly, hunger hit me and I was tickled pink to find the éclair in my hand that I had forgotten he gave me.

Taking a massive bite, I moaned as the rich chocolate frosting coated my tongue. The decadent custard filling made the éclair even better, if that was possible, as the mellow vanilla flavor played with the chocolate. *Oh, this was heaven.* Sipping the iced coffee, my body shimmied in response. I learned my lesson to never underestimate the power of an iced coffee and pastry again.

Sugar fueled my ability to stand. Reaching towards the ceiling, I stretched my limbs and spilled over into a forward fold. Alas, nearly all the tension in my body was gone. And I had the grumpy, sexy man in front of me to thank—and that kind of pissed me off. How was it fair for him to be so thoughtful and kind, and yet such a total dumbass?

Finding trusty dusty, my dust pan from the dollar store I bought the same day I bought the shop—which was surprisingly easy, thank you, Polly—I met Reid where he stood. After exchanging a brief look, we began working together without a word. Crouching, I'd hold the pan for Reid to sweep the piles into, then I would dispose of the sad, broken pieces in the large trash can. With the hazardous shards gone, we switched to rags and cleaner and began scrubbing at the paint and glaze coating the floors, tables, chairs, and walls.

Though neither of us had yet to say a word, Reid connected to the store's Bluetooth and selected a R&B playlist. Smooth vocals and soulful accompaniments filled the space as we worked together.

Intermittently, I'd sneak sideways glances at my companion. And, intermittently, I'd ignore the glances I caught Reid giving me.

Two hours and a full body of sore muscles later, the shop was almost back to life. Sure, my built-in was still mostly broken, I needed a new front window, and I'd have to replace five chairs and a shit ton of glazes, but the floor was clear of safety hazards, and there was no longer a risk of slipping or sitting in a puddle of artsy liquid.

Nearly scaring me out of my skin with the sound of clearing his voice, Reid was the first to break the silence.

"I texted a buddy from college. His uncle owns a window and roofing business, and he owes me a favor. He'll be by sometime in the next four hours to install a new window. Apparently, he has some shatterproof stuff. He said it is nearly impossible to break into, and just shy of bulletproof." Before I could tell him thanks, I could take care of it myself, he continued. "And Kara will be by in thirty with her pickup truck to help me take the big stuff to the landfill."

"What kind of favor gets you a new shatterproof shop window in four hours?"

"The kind that ends with me sharing a cell with Jared Nimbly."

I scoffed in disbelief. "Yeah, and I performed in an off-broadway show with Timothée Chalamet."

His unchanging features relayed seriousness. My jaw crashed onto the floor. Nay, it crashed *through* the floor.

"You were in jail with Jared Nimbly?" I shrieked, my voice reaching new heights. No way was Reid in jail with the world's most famous cyber hacker. After hacking the investment accounts of politicians, he posted all their trades side-by-side with press releases. The stunt proved the rampant insider trading happening, and he instantly had a target on his back. The minute he posted the information, he fled the country. Some say to a tiny island in the Philippines, others say he was sighted in Switzerland. My personal favorite theory was that he was herding penguins in Antarctica.

Reid's head bobbed, but he offered no further explanation. "What? How? When? Did he tell you about his secret plan to escape to Antarctica?" My questions rattled off my tongue without reprieve. "Do you still keep in touch? Wait! Do you think he could block Carl's number on my landline?"

Reid gave one of those bro head nods over my shoulder. Turning, I spotted a pop of fire red hair that brought a smile to my face.

"Kara!"

"Hey," the bass player said as she stepped through the massive hole where the shopwindow used to be. With a low, slow whistle, she surveyed the wreckage. "Damn, Daisy. I'm so sorry this happened."

"Me too," I sighed, happily accepting Kara's outstretched arms into a soul lifting hug. "But America's Most Wanted here has been super helpful and finagled me a new window being installed today."

Kara snorted, shaking her head. "I knew you had it bad for her."

"Kara." Reid warned.

"Reid."

I watched on as they locked eyes, having some sort of telepathic conversation. And, I'm sorry, but did she just say he had it bad for me? What did he have? A case of the "make Daisy have heart squeezing and below the belt tingly feelings then tell her I'm engaged"? Then yes, obviously, he had it bad for me. I didn't care if he'd broken up with princess posh. It didn't change what he did to me.

"Well," Kara said, drawing me from my festering thoughts. "If Reid here won't admit to anything and this thing fizzles out, you have my number."

I blushed at the wink she sent my way. "Kara, Kara, Kara. Talented, beautiful, and a flirt? Don't tempt me."

"If you two are done here, we have shit to do." Reid harrumphed, suddenly turning grumpy. His pout put a big ol' gray cloud over the light fun that I was more than happy to have as a distraction.

"Yes. We clean. Pick up heavy stuff." I grunted, matching his gruff tone.

Kara joined in, furrowing her brow and faking a comical scowl. "Throw in truck. Take to dump. Pick up women." Ignoring us, he hefted a table that had a leg missing and its frame bent, supporting it on top of his shoulder. "Okay, okay. Jeeze Superman." Shaking her head, Kara picked up the back of a chair that had snapped off and followed behind grumpy Reid.

twenty-two
daisy

ALONE AGAIN, MY TUMMY rumbled. "Okay, yes. I will feed you something other than sugar." I spoke to myself as I walked back up to my apartment. Contemplating for a moment, I tried to decide if I should leave the shop unattended, then I realized it probably didn't matter. Most of everything was destroyed, anyway.

Ellie's face flashed on my phone screen. With ranch dressing coating my fingers, I tossed another baby carrot in my mouth before answering the video call with my pinky.

"Oh my god, Daisy! Are you alright?" Ellie shrieked, skipping the niceties.

"My shop isn't, but I am," I said, willing a small smile. "You know me. I'll pull through. Hey, how did you find out?"

"Reid texted me," *motherfucker,* "and Mrs. Hudson. Word has spread all around town."

Nodding, I washed my hands and took in the information. Cool. Super stoked. Loved that for me.

"Theo is checking flights out for tonight."

"What? No, Elle's. Do not come home early because of this." Guilt racked my insides. I loved Ellie, and my heart was so full knowing she would come to my rescue like that, but I didn't want her to. She deserved this after the last year she's had.

Chewing the inside of her cheek, I could tell she was contemplating it. "But who's going to stay with you? I know you sure as hell aren't leaving your apartment. Macy Shivers herself could beg you, and you'd still dig your heels in and call her a wimp. But you shouldn't be alone. I don't want you alone. Oh wait! What about Reid?"

Rolling my eyes, I scoffed. "No."

"Daisy." Ellie warned. "If there isn't anything going on with you two, then why not?"

Popping my head out of my apartment door, I strained my ears. Once satisfied there was no one downstairs, I sighed with resignation. "Okay," I started, my voice low. "Yes, there *was* something between us. But there isn't now. So, it would just be awkward."

"I knew it!" Ellie shrieked. "Pay up Emerson! Daisy and Reid had a thing!" Theo then came into frame, slapping a crisp twenty into Ellie's outstretched hand.

"You bet on me?"

"Yep, I knew there was something going on. Theo kept telling me to let it go, but I know you. What I don't know is why you didn't tell me."

"There was nothing to tell at first." I shrugged. "We just became friendly, then the next thing I know we're kissing, and he stops us to tell me he's engaged."

"Engaged!" Ellie's eyes threatened to pop from her skull. "To the Liz girl?"

"Well, technically not engaged, but close enough."

"I heard they broke up, though." A clang downstairs made me jump, dropping my phone. "What happened?"

Reid's voice floated up the staircase. "Daisy?"

"Reid's back," I whisper into the phone.

"Reid's there?" Ellie asked, a smug look playing on her face.

"Don't even." I point a finger at her through the video. "I'll talk to you later. Love you."

"Love you."

"Coming!" I shouted back down to Reid as I ended the call.

Emerging from the stairs, I see that not only was Reid back, but he also brought with him a toolbox.

"What's this?" I eyed the black rectangular case.

"Tools."

"Yes, I can see that. The question is why?" Just then, a small framed, broad-shouldered woman stomped in, weighted down by the sawhorse hitched on her hip. "Marley?" I questioned, taking in the appearance of the local woodworker.

"Hey Daze. Ran into Reid at the dump and heard about your trouble. We'll get your shelves fixed back up in no time." With her hands on both her hips, she stood in a total power pose. Her eyes sparkled with the challenge in front of her.

Stuttering, I felt my cheeks heat. Wow. That may have been the first time in my life my cheeks ever heated. "No, please. You don't have to do that."

Putting her hand up, Marley firmly shook her head. "I want to. We take care of our own here. I hoped you would have known that by now."

Blinking away threatening tears, I nodded in thanks, and she understood. Years spent alone and taking care of myself made moments like these, when people *cared*, hard.

Halfway through replacing and repairing the broken shelves, the window installation team arrived. As a lame attempt at thanking them for their massive favors, I ordered pizzas, sandwiches, and beers. The laughter that flowed fueled my recovery. The disaster of this morning was slowly withering away as my community came in to help.

Nearly every person who stopped by mentioned Reid's name. Some because he had spoken to them, asking them to stop by, others because they were admiring his glistening body. Sweat pricked at his shirt, making it cling to his form, and all the lifting he'd done gave his muscles a decent pump. I was going to have to mop up after everyone left, because the collective drool was flooding the place.

Sitting next to me on the bottom step of my staircase, Reid tipped back his beer. I watched as his throat bobbed and sweat trickled down over his temple. "Hey, thank you for everything today. You have no idea what this means to me."

"Tell me." His reply was simple, but effective all the same. My walls came down easily around him.

Sighing, I leaned back onto my hands. Watching the crew around us work, my heart swelled. "I'm okay being alone. I've gotten by on my own for a while. Since I was a child. No matter the situation, I knew that when my mom let me down, at least I could count on myself. That didn't mean it was easy, though. Usually, it took a lot of time, money, and curse words. To be shown what it means to have a community is as equally fulfilling as it is heartbreaking. My heart aches for twelve-year-old me who volunteered at a thrift store for a free meal, and my heart swells knowing that, that twelve-year-old girl grew up to find herself somewhere she'd never have to worry about that again. And I have you to thank."

His face was unreadable as he soaked in my words. "They would have shown up for you, with or without me."

"Maybe. But thanks to you, it wasn't a question. Now, nearly ten hours after one of the worst mornings of my life, my shop is almost completely repaired."

"Well, then, you're welcome." Turning to me, he gave the sweetest, widest grin. It was easier to convince myself I hated him when we were going toe-to-toe. But, in this vulnerable moment, I saw him. I saw the Reid I knew. And shit. All those feelings I once had were still there.

Clearing his throat, he set his beer down. "I don't mean to be overbearing..."

I could sense the *but* coming, and I didn't want to lose this moment. "Then don't be."

He chuckled, ruffling a hand through his hair. "I was going to say, I don't mean to be overbearing, but are you going to have anyone stay with you? Kendrick said you don't want to leave your shop, but you really shouldn't be—alone." He tripped over the last word, my confession over this morning hanging silently over us.

"I appreciate the concern, but I'll be just fine." I drew my lips into a tight line. Yes, there we go. Frustrate me, Reid, so I can go back to hating you.

"I know you're a badass who can take care of herself, but that doesn't change what has happened here, or that there is someone hell bent on making your life miserable."

"Don't you think I know that?" Exhaustion hit me like a truck. I was so tired of this; of having to watch my back and being scared for my life. "Golly, gee. The broken glass and lost art were all planned. Part of my new aesthetic. What d'ya think?"

"Har har. Listen, I'm not implying anything. I'm just concerned."

"I'm sorry," my shoulders slumped. He didn't deserve my anger. This man not only stood by my side, but also took the reins. Between that and the muscle show, my head was spinning. Damn it. "You're right, I'm just a little frazzled. This has been a lot."

Silence took back over, and I sighed.

"Ellie and Theo are visiting her family in Idaho. Jake and Penny rented a boat house and are incommunicado for another week. There isn't anyone else I trust enough to stick with me."

Being alone was something I had mastered. Originally, it started as a way to be in control of myself. But it turned into a life where I only had so many people I could depend on. Although, Chestnut Hills was showing me that wasn't true—there were plenty of people around who would step up in a time of need.

"What about me?" Reid asked.

I blinked rapidly at him. "What about you?"

"Why don't I stay with you?"

"Because," I scoffed. "Because..." I searched for a reason. "Because, because. That's why."

"Solid reasoning. Might I interest you in even more solid reasoning of why I should: I cook a mean eggplant parmesan, I'm very tidy, and my 6' 5" fits perfectly on a couch," he listed off as he counted with his fingers. I clamped my lips shut to suppress the smile that threatened at the thought of Reid cramped on my purple velvety couch.

"Eggplant makes me gag, I'm a hot mess, and though I would love nothing more than to make you suffer through a night on my couch, my conscious is a bigger person than me."

"I'll make it chicken parmesan, you are definitely hot, but not a mess, and I would suffer through worse if it meant I got to make sure you were safe. Also...I'll tell you the story about sharing a cell with Jared Nimbly."

Damnit, that was good reasoning. My inclination to agree with him had nothing to do with the flip my stomach did when he complimented me or spoke of his desire to keep me safe.

"You make a compelling argument, Flores. One night," I offered.

"Until the creep is behind bars," he countered.

"That could be years, if ever!"

"Fine by me," he flashed a smile.

"Three nights."

"Three months."

"Reid," I warned.

"Daisy," he flirted.

"A week."

"Three weeks."

"You're insane."

"Apparently I am, when it comes to you." This time he winked, and my insides turned to putty. I wasn't sure of his end game, but there were worse things than having Reid Flores in my home.

Just as he did earlier, before running out to grab breakfast, he placed another gentle kiss on my forehead. I watched after in awe as he jogged back up to Marley, taking her position, holding a shelf in place while she secured the brackets.

I had called Liam, Calley, and Polly earlier to let them know what happened. All had offered to come in and help, but I declined. Our shop was already full of helping hands. Instead, I gave them the day to relax and double check their home security systems. Not that I thought that anything would happen to them, but you know. Precaution.

Now, I had to call my clients, cancel classes for the next two days, and apologize for any broken pottery pieces. Just as Ellie said, word was already around town and every client already knew what was coming. Luckily, I had the greatest bunch of clients, and every single person declined to take payment for their broken consignment pieces.

Listening to a client tell me about wanting to host a pottery night with her church group, I restrained myself, trying to keep my mouth from dropping as I watched Reid bend at the waist. His cute butt called me—I wanted to slap it. With him staying with me, maybe I would indulge in a little fun. I deserved it.

Between that, and the high I was riding from the kindness of my town, I reminded myself that life was pretty good.

Ending my last call, I sent a text off to Ellie.

Daisy

DO NOT BOOK A FLIGHT. I WILL DISOWN YOU.

Reid is going to stay with me.

Ellie

Excellent.

Daisy

I can hear your maniacal laughter from across the country.

twenty-three

reid

DAMN. DAISY REALLY WASN'T exaggerating when she said I'd be miserable on the couch. Purple and plush, it looked deceivingly comfortable. But for the third morning in a row, I woke with a sharp pain in my neck and a migraine that took two cups of coffee to numb.

Mentally, I added buying an air mattress to my to-do list.

From my pained position on the couch, I looked around, assessing the second-floor apartment against the person I knew Daisy to be. And it fit her down to the spoons with frog shaped bowls. They weren't nearly as functional to eat off of as a normal person spoon was, but it made sense Daisy owned them.

The ceiling above the couch was pink. It might have been too much had she not kept the walls an ivory white like she did. One might think it was an attempt to even out the explosion of color her apartment was. Yet, that blip of perceived evenness was quickly overshadowed with neon rainbow-colored squiggly shelves in green, pink, and orange.

An airy voice carried down the hall, humming a bright tune.

"Morning," Daisy sang. I grunted in response, swinging my feet over the side and sitting up. "Ready to give up yet, stubborn man?" she asked.

"Give up what?"

"Sleeping here," she said over the lip of her coffee mug. "I told you that the couch was uncomfortable for sleeping."

"Nice try, but I'm staying until this Carl guy is gone or someone else can come take my place. Besides, my roommate's girlfriend just moved in. Figured I'd give them some space."

She assessed me with a hum. "For being so grumpy all the time, I thought maybe you might be happier in the mornings. Looks like it's a 24/7 thing."

"For being so exuberant all the time, I thought you'd be able to find the bright side of having a good-looking man like me sleep on your couch."

"Good looking man? Where?"

"Let's not pretend you haven't been taking any chance you can get to oogle me." I deadpanned. Standing, I stretched, reaching my hands to the ceiling. Daisy lifted her mug to obstruct her view, and I did nothing to hide the smile that stretched across my face.

Padding to the kitchen, I filled a mug of coffee for myself. We stared at each other over our mugs for a moment before she set hers down, retreating down the hallway.

The sound of the shower coming to life was quickly drowned out by loud music coming from her Bluetooth speaker. Quickly, I dressed myself and grabbed my laptop bag. On a swivel, I almost missed the cracked bathroom door, giving a perfect view of the vanity mirror.

Only for a second I watched her shrug off her nightshirt, revealing her bare back. Her blonde locks fell over her shoulder, but as she brought them back behind her, they fell long. My brain completed the image of the tips brushing the curve of her ass. Quickly, I averted my eyes and walked out the front door.

The weekly meeting was bland, and I made a small to-do list in my calendar for the day, remembering to add *get an air mattress* to the list.

Assessing my remaining meetings for the rest of the week, an invitation popped into my inbox.

Lunch with Your Mother

I nearly fell out of my chair at the notification and spent a few minutes taking in my surroundings, trying to confirm this was real life. Opening the invite, I read the passive-aggressive message.

Since you cannot be bothered to answer your phone or return my calls, I had to ask little Paul down the street to teach me how to do this. You should be ashamed. See you at noon.

"Little Paul" was a nineteen-year-old college student home for summer who lived down the street. Assessing that fact and my feelings towards her message, I decided that no, I wasn't ashamed. In place of where shame would have lived, I felt warmth. Pride stood firmly in its place and I recognized that maybe this was it, maybe it was finally time that I fully lived for myself. With that thought, I was antsy to return to my temporary home and walk-in to see Daisy. Fully aware of what had transpired with us over the last few months, I knew I had to win her trust back. I was struck with the importance of winning her trust back, and it far outweighed marrying a woman I couldn't stand so my cheating father could get away with betraying my mom.

I accepted the invite, clarifying we'd be meeting at Salsas. Mom felt the vibrant colors and murals brought the value of the food down. I felt that if I was going to get through this conversation I'd been avoiding, I'd need free chips and salsa—a lot of free chips and salsa.

Greeted with a kiss on each cheek, my mom and I sat across from each other in the wooden booth. Greedily, I dove into the chips, scooping a large glop of salsa with it.

"Reid, have a little poise," mom instructed.

"I have plenty of poise," I said, talking with my mouth full. Nerves were vibrating through every limb. I may have been a stoic man, one people thought was unwavering, but when it came to my mom, that became challenging. She had the power to change my mind, but I had to remind myself that I was in control here.

"I suppose you know why I have been calling, and I suppose I know why you have not been answering," she sipped from her lemon water and played with a chip in her hands.

"I suppose," was all I could muster.

Chewing in silence, I watched her twirl the fried tortilla between her hands. Tension grew between us, drawing attention to the silence that sat in place of what we each wanted to say. Our food was brought out—a massive chimichanga for me and a chicken salad for mom—and instead of eating, she moved to fidget with her silverware.

"Mom," I started, unable to bear watching her struggle anymore.

"No, darling. Let me start, please," she interrupted. "I—I am trying to find the words." She took another sip of her water and when she looked at me, I realized she was holding back tears.

"As you know, I married your father right out of college. We never explored anything outside of each other, outside of the expectations placed on us. Your father, well, he was well off, put together. I never had the chest crushing feeling with him, but when I saw the security a life with him would provide, I was more than happy to ignore that.

"Please know, I love you very much, and your father. I regret nothing when it comes to you and the life I built, but I do regret putting love in the backseat when I had a chance to design what my life would turn out to be. I would not change a thing if it meant I would lose you, but I decided I cannot let you make the same mistake.

"Sweetheart, I realized that if there is one thing I want for you, it is for you to be with someone you love. Create a life you are proud of and know you did it for no one else but yourself."

Reaching across the table, I grabbed her hand and gave it a reassuring squeeze.

"I had no idea, mom," I finally said. "I'm so sorry."

"Quite alright, dear. I have made my way. Time to make yours. Just make it in a way that when you are my age, you look back and know that you made the right choice. I want you to look back when you are old and gray and know you lived a life of love and have no regrets."

The words struck my core—no regrets. What did no regrets look like for me?

"Mom, I have something to tell you...I play the drums."

Her eyebrows flew behind her puffed bangs. "The drums?"

"Yes. I'm in a band. We play gigs around town and we're pretty good. It's a hobby of mine, and I wanted to share that with you."

"Wh-what? Well, it's not quite the piano or cello, but tha-that is lovely, dear," she patted my hand, a pained smile on her face.

"I don't think I've ever heard you stutter before," I laughed. In response, she let out a sharp bark. We both laughed in surprise at that, and she lost herself in a fit of giggles.

"Oh dear," she swiped at a tear, "I love you."

"I love you, mom."

twenty-four

daisy

Something was different.

It wasn't the fancy new window, or barren, freshly stained shelves. It wasn't the loss of money, or whispered words when I walked down the street, or the gawkers who walked past my storefront.

There was a funny feeling in the air that settled in my bones. The feeling gave me a sense of security and optimism. This mess was temporary, and there were new beginnings on the horizon. I could feel it.

Since the incident, I hadn't had a threatening call yet. Granted, it had only been a few days, but the peace was welcomed. And tonight, with Polly helping Calley with running the store, and half of my leftover panini calling my name, I was going to sit back, put my feet up, and relax.

My apartment door creaked open, and I was greeted with darkness. Deepening purples and blues had taken over the night sky outside as I walked home. Now, without a light on inside, I couldn't see a thing. But I could feel that something had shifted. The Feng Shui of it all was changed. Flipping the switch on the wall next to me, no light shined. *Damn it. I must've unplugged the lamp when I was vacuuming earlier.*

With my arms outstretched, I tentatively walked into the space. Outlining the corner of the room should have been my bulbus floor lap. It sounded weirder than it was, but it was a distinct shape that would help me get my bearings *and* grant me light.

"Ahhhh," my scream was cut off as the wind was knocked out of me. Something unusual caught my foot and I fell, a large, bouncy thing saving me from completely wiping out. Struggling to right myself, I heard the bathroom door open, accompanied by a deep curse. Strong hands wrapped around my arms, pulling me to my feet.

"Shit, sorry Daze," Reid apologized. Though I couldn't see his face, his deep tone was familiar.

The kitchen light came to life and there he was, at the switch in the hallway, a towel low on his hips. He continued to talk, but I was struggling to process what he was saying when all I could see was chest. More specifically, a broad chest with a light spattering of dark hair covered in droplets of water glistening as they slid down.

A sound was all I could muster in response. "Huh?"

"Eyes up here, baby," he said coyly. I looked up and blinked to clear away the lust. A smirk played at his lips, as if he could smell the shift in my hormones at the sight of his chiseled body.

"Uh...you...what...fall...huh?" My arms accompanied my jumbled thoughts, flailing around as I attempted to make sense of the situation.

"Sorry about that." He reached up, scratching his head. His bicep flexed with the motion, and I swallowed back the drool. His other hand held the towel closed—barely—around his waist, and I made sure not to stare. "I couldn't take another night on the couch, so I got an air mattress. I hope that's alright with you."

"Sure," I went with the easiest answer so I could get away from whatever was happening with me and my clear loss of communication abilities.

Catching me off guard, he motioned to the kitchen. "Have any plans for dinner?" he asked.

"The other half of my lunch has been calling my name."

"I thought I'd make good on my offer of chicken parmesan, if you're interested? I have breadsticks to go with it."

"Breadsticks? Well, then, obviously, yes. I am definitely interested."

"Great."

"Great."

Damn it, those dimples. Water dripped off the tips of his unkempt hair, sliding down his rippled stomach. My lady bits pulsed at the sight. What was happening here? This was exactly why I didn't want him staying here.

Turning around, I walked away, trying to busy myself and ignore the sounds of him returning to the bathroom. Was he naked in there? *Of course,* he was naked.

I just needed to stop thinking about it.

Laid out on the new air mattress, which was delightfully comfortable, I watched as Reid worked in the kitchen. He was capable and graceful when he was working on my shop the other day. In the kitchen, he was methodical, intentional, and passionate. He slowly moved between his meticulously set stations. Chicken, into egg wash, into breadcrumbs, into frying pan, then stir the sauce. My head felt dizzy watching him move back and forth. Yet, he did it with ease. It was hypnotic, with the sounds of Nora Jones flitting through the Bluetooth speaker.

Silently, he brought me a drink. In jeans and a fitted tee, he had also thrown a hand towel thrown over his shoulder. He was a tempting picture of domesticity.

"What's this?" I asked, looking into the deep crimson liquid with a leafy green garnish. Tart and fruity scents floated to me from the glass, accented with crispness from the effervescence of the drink. Underneath that, there was a calming aroma of...*was that mint?*

"Virgin blackberry mojito," he responded, eyes already focused back on the pot of sauce.

Taking a sip, the fizzy, tart, sweet, minty goodness coated my tongue. I groaned in appreciation of the deliciousness and happily sipped while I watched the sexy chef at work. An hour later, I was sitting cross-legged on the mattress while Reid laid out on the side, his elbow propping him up. We quietly took our first bites of our dinner, and I immediately blushed after releasing an embarrassing moan.

"Accountant, drummer, and now mixologist and chef? What can't you do?" I asked, my mouth full of chicken.

"Get this girl, sorry, woman, I like to give me a second chance," he said, eyeing me.

"I wasn't aware you were wanting one."

"I wasn't talking about you," he said. Silence hung heavily as we stared at each other down before he cracked a smile, prompting me to throw a breadstick at him. "Still want to hear about the time I met Jared Nimbly? It's not that interesting, but I think it makes me look pretty good."

My eyebrow quirked at that. "Hmm," I hummed. "I'll be the judge of that. Lay it on me."

"Okay," he promptly took a bite of the breadstick I had thrown at him. "So, I was at a basketball game with Seth, a buddy from college. Go Spurs. Because of the popularity of the teams, these tickets were lottery based. It was blind luck we got seated next to his crush. They're hitting it off, we're all making conversation, and at the end of the third quarter he finally got the courage to ask her out. And she said no."

My jaw dropped. "I thought this was going somewhere sweet."

"It is, keep listening, Bloom. So, she says no, but I can't have that. Seth is a great guy, and he'd been pining after this girl for months. In accordance with my best friend duties, I interject and ask her to make a bet. She had been talking to her friend about the streaker at the football game a few months before, and how she was bummed she missed it. So, naturally, I bet that if there was a streaker, she would go on a date with Seth. She agreed, and there were only five minutes left in the last quarter with no streaker in sight. What is there left for me to do but to excuse myself, make my way to the floor, drop trousers, and run?"

Virgin Blackberry Mojito went spraying everywhere. The mattress, my plate, his face. Visions of Reid, naked and running across a basketball court in a stadium full of people, danced in my head. I was so enthralled with imagining the scene; I didn't even process that I had just stained everything within a four-foot radius with my spittle.

"I am so sorry." I laughed, a hand flying to cover my mouth.

"It's a good story," he laughed with me, dabbing at the purple tinted spots on his new air mattress. "Well, Seth got the date, and I got arrested for public nudity. But I wasn't actually nude, nude. I was in my boxers. A technicality that got me out, but not before being placed in a cell with Jared Nimbly. Back then, he wasn't the Jared Nimbly we know today. He'd just been arrested for hacking into the local public school system and deleting everyone's lunch debts, but they didn't have enough evidence to make it stick, so it's not really well known."

"Holy shit." I processed my shock from the story before acquiescing. "Alright, you have dutifully fulfilled your part of the deal. That story was worth having you invade my space."

"Invade?" he scoffed. "Since I seem to be an inconvenience, I'll just trash the rest of these inconvenient bread sticks."

"Touch the breadsticks and die." Glancing at the clock, I realized it was nearly nine. Unprepared for the night to end, I had an idea. "If you're up to it, I want to test the theory that you can do anything..." I trailed off in a question, biting my lip. "Come downstairs with me."

Without waiting for his response, I shot up from the mattress. Before opening the front door and descending the stairs, I snagged my studio keys from the pink tiger butt key hook by my front door. A second pair of footsteps echoed off the walls as he followed behind.

Shutters were drawn over the windows, deepening the darkness of the closed storefront. With the flip of a switch, the space came to life. Anticipation made my hands shake as the key clicked open the two padlocks that separated the storefront from the studio space.

Luckily, I had the foresight to put in the extra barrier between the two rooms. Even when Ellie told me I was being overly cautious, I knew there was a reason I felt I had to do it in my gut. Had the door not been there, Carl would've destroyed my precious wheels too. The cost to replace those would have been upwards of eighteen thousand, and lord knew my credit limit was only so high.

Reid let out a low whistle as eight vacant pottery wheels came into view as I pushed the heavy door open. *My precious.* I was no better than Gollum himself.

I directed Reid to the closest wheel. "Sit." His stare bore into my back as I worked on autopilot, filling a bowl of water. Movements that were second nature to me had become anxious, each flex of a muscle requiring full attention.

My blue pottery apron draped over my slight frame, and I worked to cut a sizeable chuck of pottery clay. Reid listened intently as I explained the act of wedging the clay, working on getting all the air bubbles out.

"Do I need one of those?" he asked, motioning to my apron.

"Nah, you can just take your shirt off—oh—okay." I stuttered as he removed his shirt in one swift motion, pulling it over his head. I was just joking, but this was just fine, too. *Damn it, that chest.*

I used every bit of self-restraint, coaching myself that whatever I did, *do not look. Do not gape. Do not drool.* Walking over, I placed the clay firmly on the bat and began pointing out the parts of the wheel. "Here is your foot petal. This controls the speed. This is the bat, holding the clay. It's removable. This is the wheel head, and this is the splash pan. Here is a bucket of water which we'll need to get your hands wet."

Mischief twinkled in his eye. "Are we about to do this? Are you going to Patrick Swayze me?"

"You wish you were Demi Moore." I scoffed. "Now, take your hands and begin tapping the clay to the center while pressing the foot petal slowly."

At glacier speed, the wheel began moving. Tentatively, he flattened his hand and tapped at the mound.

"Great, now get your hands wet—perfect. Okay, here comes the fun part." I held my breath as my chest pressed against his back, my heartbeat thrumming between us. Helping him into position, I pulled in his elbows tightly against his body. Electricity sparked as I slid my hands down his forearms, his body tensing under my touch.

"When you feel it start to give, slowly but firmly squeeze the clay as you come up." My hands rested on his, guiding him to apply pressure where needed.

"Are we still talking about clay?" he asked, raising an eyebrow.

"Shhh, hotshot. I want you to focus. You said you like numbers because of their predictability and the degree of control. Here you get to control, but without the predictability. There are so many factors that can influence the outcome—what type of clay you use, how much water you use, where you put pressure, how much pressure you use."

Dutifully, he listened as I guided him through the steps. His playfulness faded and the serious, determined Reid I knew took over. I knew I'd lost him when his brow furrowed in concentration, and I thought maybe it was for the best we quickly dampen the sexual tension that had been brewing between us. His forearms flexed with the movement, and I pretended not to notice his biceps flexed against his bare expanse of chest.

"Now, thin out the wall. Pull, squeeze and lift with your fingertips," I watched him flawlessly do the first pull, pleasantly surprised. And, admittedly, surprisingly, disappointed by the lack of a dirty joke. "Go back to the base and thin out more. You want to get to your desired thickness before pulling back up."

Slowly, he pulled up his fingertips, keeping his light touch. The tenderness he moved with stirred something in me. Behind his rigidness, I saw his attentiveness, the kindness that had to exist in movement like that. His gaze shot up to me, and I worried I had said that out loud.

"Shit," he cursed just as a large tear ripped through the wall of clay and it flopped over.

The incident startled him in a way that made his foot slam on the petal and the clay spun aggressively. The uneven rip began flinging bits of clay along. Splashes of water were whipped off in every direction.

"Lesson one, keep your eyes on the clay, newbie." I laughed.

Unsuccessfully, he wiped at a bit of clay that had landed on his cheek. His stained hand left an even more noticeable mark. Overwhelming joy bubbled from the base of belly, and I couldn't stop the giggle. He looked at me in disbelief before dipping his hand in the water and flicking in my direction.

Cool water speckled my already sensitive skin, and I shouted in surprise. Wetting my hand, I did the same to him. Somehow, we drew closer together. The feet between us turned into inches that turned into a breath. As I felt the warmth of his body radiating off him, I realized we were nearly chest to chest. Taking advantage of the opportunity, he took a pinch of clay and smeared it on my cheek. Spotting a chunk of clay that had flown off onto the table next to me, I grabbed it and smeared it across the firm expanse of his chest.

Our points of connection sparked. The sensation sent us both into a high, our breaths hitching and our eyes widening.

Before I could blink, his mouth was on mine. The tidal wave of pleasure beckoned me to submit. Powerless against the pull, I surrendered, opening my mouth to him. Groaning in acceptance, he crowded me. Our feet worked in time as I walked back, stopping when the work bench pressed into my back. We moved as one, our mouths refusing to separate. A symphony played between our touches, our mouths keeping time in their own waltz.

My hands moved on their own accord, seeking more like a fly to honey. My fingers threaded his hair, tugging at the roots as I wordlessly begged for more. I allowed him to remove my apron as his firm hands roamed my body. His thickening member pressed against my stomach, letting me know he was as hungry for me as I was for him.

A fervor took over. I couldn't breathe, I couldn't move, I couldn't think. I could only seek to quell the hunger that tore at my belly. A quip of excitement slipped past my lips as he firmly gripped my ass and hefted me onto the workbench.

Clay smeared as my hands roamed, unconscious of the mess. He looked like a work of art; a God carved into marble. And. Oh. My. God. I thought I might explode if I didn't feel every inch of him as quickly as possible. Wetness pooled between my legs, surging me to unbuckle his belt.

His hands brushed my mid-drift, coasting higher beneath my shirt. With a silent, disapproving nod, I jumped off the bench and dropped to my knees.

"Lesson two, I like to be the lead." I said, unzipping his pants slowly as I held eye contact. His length was highlighted as he strained against his boxer briefs and I tugged his jeans down to his ankles. I salivated, both with excitement and pride, knowing that I drove him as wild as he drove me.

My fingernails scraped against him as they begged for control over his waistband. Impatient to unveil him, I whined when he pulled me back to my feet. "What if I like to be the lead?" he asked, his eyes hooded.

"Tough luck." With a seductive smile, I placed his hands on the counter behind me. "Stay," I directed as I slithered back down. Before he could stop me again, I yanked his boxers down and stared in awe as he sprang free.

"Okay, just this one time," he said in total weakness as his head dropped in resignation.

I shushed him before licking the bead of moisture that hung from the tip. The salty, sweet taste of him was intoxicating. I wanted more. He moaned as I swirled my tongue around the head of his cock. And that moan—*holy shit.*

Drawing back, I looked up at him and took in his total vulnerability. His eyes were closed as his head hung, his breathing was shallow, and his fingers clenched the counter as if he was gripping onto his last drop of sanity.

He opened his eyes at my withdrawal. Locking eyes, I held his gaze as I slowly took his hard length into my mouth. Inch by inch, it slid down my throat, hitting a spot that made my eyes water. Just as slowly,

I pulled him back out and gave a hard suck at the tip, releasing him with a *pop*.

"Fuck," he breathed, his eyes rolling into the back of his head.

I repeated the process, once, twice, thrice, until I was sure he was going to lose his mind. My name was on the tip of his tongue as he begged me for more, and I'd never felt more powerful. There was something to be said about having a man like Reid at the mercy of my total control.

"Daisy, please, I want to—I want to feel you," he begged, reaching down.

I swatted his hand away, my mouth full. "Not yet. I want this."

A moment barely passed before I felt him tense under my fingertips wrapped around his thighs. Pulling him in deep, I swallowed, working my throat around him. With a guttural moan, he pulsed. His seed coated the back of my throat as I licked him clean.

Standing, I greeted him with a smile. Sweat beaded his forehead, and his eyes were heavy. I wrapped my hands around his neck as I waited for him to look at me. When he did, he stroked my cheek with his thumb and kissed my forehead.

"You're going to be the death of me, Daisy Bloom."

twenty-five

daisy

WE CLEANED AND JOKED and laughed and kissed our way back upstairs. It was getting late, but we couldn't separate ourselves from each other, having finally surrendered to the pull we felt. His arms were wrapped lazily around my waist as I scooped peach cobbler—peach cobbler that he had made—into a set of bowls, accompanied by a healthy scoop of ice cream.

"If this peach cobbler is half as good as your chicken parmesan, you get to sleep in my bed tonight," I said, taking a big bite of the caramel goodness.

"I had some plans for the bed. And if you're going to hang it all on my world-famous peach cobbler, I might as well get started."

I moaned at the sweetness coating my tongue, mixed with the cool creaminess of the ice cream. At the same time, he placed a kiss on the nape of my neck while lifting the hem of my shirt. His thumb brushed the curve of my breast. The graze, though soft, burned me to my core. I arched into his touch.

"Okay, you win." I said, picking up both bowls and leading the way to my bedroom.

"Was it the kiss?" he called after me.

"Silly boy. It was the peach cobbler."

Pillows propped us up, side by side, shoulders touching, as we took mirrored bites of our dessert, savoring the peace of our companion'd silence. Wetness trickled down my neck and I looked to find a white trail making its way down to the center of my breasts. A spoon hovered next to my head, held by a smug Reid.

"Oops," the seduction of his smile was only intensified by his dark eyes. "Let me get that for you."

He flatted his tongue against my chest and made slow, deliberate moves, lapping at the mess. The sensation of his mouth on me made my breath falter. Slowly, he followed the sweet trail to the valley between my breasts.

"Sorry, I need to get in there to make sure I do a thorough clean-up job. Remove this, please," he asked, lifting my shirt off, revealing a hot pink satin bra. My already hardened nipples strained against the fabric, the lack of padding calling more attention to it.

He nipped at the stiff peak through the thin satin barrier. I gasped at the surprise sensation. Refocusing on the dripping ice cream, he continued licking and kissing his way down to where the cream had melted down to the waist of my jeans. In anticipation, I panted, my breaths coming in hard, brief spurts.

The look in his eyes was devilish as he looked up, peaking his tongue under the waist of my underwear then kissing his way back up. "I think I got it all," he smiled, rolling back to his side.

I sat up and unclasped my bra, giving myself a pat on the back when I watched his pupils dilate to the size of saucers. Tossing the pink satin to the side, I used my finger to scoop up the fruity caramel of the cobbler and rubbed it slowly around each nipple.

"You missed some," I purred.

Laying me back down, he repositioned himself over my heaving body. He lowered his head, and pleasure surged through me as he moved his mouth over my breast. Lapping at the peak, he pulled it into his mouth. Sucking, biting, then licking away the hurt, he worked me into putty.

The need to have him closer to me took over. Threading my hands through his hair, I pulled him tighter to me. Hungrily, he moved his mouth to the other breast while kneading the abandoned one with his hand. The rough pad of his thumb rubbed against the already sensitive peak. Just as he nipped at the nipple in his mouth, he roughly pinched the other, causing me to arch into his touch and scream in ecstasy.

Heat rapidly built in my core. My chest felt on fire as I tried to catch my breath. The mound between my thighs was pulsing with need, and I tried pushing my legs together to ease the impending combustion.

"Uh-huh," he mumbled, his mouth still on me. Abandoning my breast, I whimpered as he used his hand to push my legs apart.

Electricity pulsed through me as he reached his hand under the waist of my pants. I'd had sexual partners, I did the sex regularly, but this. *This.* My body craved his, my nerves tightened and tingled under his attention. *Get it together,* I chastised myself when I almost lost all composure as he stroked me through my satin panties.

I was about to come from over the panty stuff. Have mercy.

Removing his hand, he used it to unbutton and unzip my pants. With a *pop*, he released my straining nipple from his mouth. Before I could protest, I thought better of it as I watched him yank my jeans off and kneel before me.

I winced at the faded white scar that cut across my left thigh and forced myself to stay focused on the sexy as hell man between my legs. What typically served as a stinging reminder of my past was irrelevant when I had a broody Adonis kissing my ankles.

His hands explored up my calf, and I opened wider to him. He growled in appreciation. The sensation of him kissing up the inside of my thighs made my heart palpitate. The light touches of his lips were starkly contrasted by the brush of his beard. I squirmed under his attention as he made his way up. Lost in the pleasure, I didn't realize he'd made his way until his hot breath seeped through the thin fabric of my panties.

"Pl—please," I asked breathlessly. He placed a light kiss on the fabric right on top of my sensitive nub and I almost came at the friction. "For the love of all things holy, please, Reid!" I shouted.

With a wicked smile, he hooked a finger on the side of my panties and tugged the fabric to the side. There was no hesitation or lightness about him as he dove in, tasting me, eating me up. Harshly, he licked, flicked and sucked.

He was pure power, control, and sin.

The ferocity caught me off guard. A jolt of electricity surged my body, and I arched into him. The sound of fabric ripping filled the space. My torn underwear quickly flew to the other side of the room. Flattening his tongue, he ran it along my slit. The intentional motion was sensual, catching me off guard in contrast to the hungry devouring of my clit. I hooked my legs over his shoulders and the fear of suffocating him quickly dissipated the minute he thrusted a finger in my entrance.

"Reid, I'm—I'm gonna..." I panted.

"Come. Come for me Daisy. I want to taste it all," he declared as he added another finger, thrusting deeply into me.

The tension at the base of my spine gathered. Electricity shot through every limb. I screamed as I tugged on his hair and curled my toes. Spasms rocked my body as I shouted his name. His mouth stayed on me until the overwhelming sensation was too much. Tugging at his ends, I pulled him away as I came down from my high. Returning to kissing my inner thigh, I managed to take a few deep breaths during the reprieve.

Kissing his way back to my mouth, I felt his hardened cock press against me through his god forsaken jeans. Our lips collided, and I reached for him. Gripping his shaft beneath his boxer briefs, I began tugging.

"Daisy, I can't get enough of you," he whispered lightly. "Your touch drives me wild."

We kissed deeply as he allowed me to shove his pants and underwear down, using my feet as leverage. Even though I'd seen him nearly an hour ago, his length still shocked me. Remnants of clay still speckled his chest when he broke away momentarily to pull his shirt off. Hot diggity dog. This man was hot.

Each of us, bare in our nakedness, stared at each other. He reminded me of a lion on the prowl as he bent over to all fours and climbed over me. Lining his length along my slit, he moved his hips, creating the most delicious friction. He made a move to stand, and I whimpered, wanting to drag him back on top of me.

"What-what're you doing?" I whined.

Picking through his discarded jeans, he searched frantically. "Condom."

"Bedside table," I directed breathlessly. He opened the top drawer of my adorably purple squiggle shaped nightstand and pulled out a half empty bulk sized box.

"I'm going to pretend I don't notice that this is half empty—a seventy-five count Daisy!" he exclaimed, getting distracted by entirely the wrong thing.

"Don't be weird. A girl has needs, and right now, I need you."

His eyes darkened at my blunt declaration. *That's more like it.* Tearing an aluminum packet from a strip of the like, his eyes bore into me. "Touch yourself for me," he demanded as he ripped the package with his teeth. Tapping my foot with a hand, he motioned for me to open up, letting me know he wanted to see more. "Wider."

Boldly, I trailed my hand down my stomach to my core and began making lazy circles around my still swollen sex. Using the wetness of my arousal, I played freely with myself. My desire pooled again at the knowledge of what was to come.

Teasingly, he rolled the protection onto his thick cock. Without thinking, I bit my lip in response and gripped one of my breasts, teasing it. Tugging and pinching at my nipple, I tried to recreate the sensation of Reid, but I realized nothing would ever compare. He'd ruined me.

Eagerly, he shoved my hand out of the way and replaced it with his mouth, pulling at my taunt peak as he nudged his tip at my entrance.

Impatiently, I moved my hips to meet him. Pulling away, he tsked at me. "Lesson one for *you*, baby—patience is rewarded," he growled into my ear, nipping at the lobe.

I thrusted up towards him again, and when he moved away, I rolled us over. The bowls of discarded ice cream and cobbler clattered to the floor. We both ignored the commotion. That would be fun to clean up—*later*.

"I'd like to redirect *you* to your second lesson—I like to be the lead." Positioning myself over him, I lined his tip with my entrance again and lowered down. Inch by glorious inch, I took him in with a hiss of breath that matched his.

I panted as I moved up and down. "So. Full." A sigh of relief escaped me as he reached a spot that'd never been hit before. It was pure ecstasy.

"Daisy, baby, if you keep moving like that, I'm not going to last long," he strained, a sexy as fuck vein visible on the side of his neck.

"Well, I don't plan on stopping." I moved up and down, my pace quickening.

My head was tugged back as his hand snaked up my spine, wrapping my hair around his hand, and giving it a firm tug. Bringing a hand down my body, I worked myself while riding him, taking pleasure in the sensation of my hair being tugged and his eyes on my bouncing breasts.

Shivers racked my body as the mounting pleasure overtook me. My breaths became shallow, and I was chanting his name.

"I can feel you quivering, baby. The way your pussy grips my cock is fucking delicious," he growled. "I'm right there with you Daze."

Without warning, he moved to bite my neck, and light filled my vision. More. I needed more.

"Cover my cock in your come, Daze. I want to feel you lose control," he growled.

I felt him thicken inside me. Somehow, he became impossibly bigger. My walls tightened around him, and I felt his member pulse as he rolled his eyes back with my name on his lips. The sight and sensation made me come undone.

"Reid, oh God, Reid," I cried out in pleasure. Together we shook, enjoying the electricity that flowed between us and the mind-blowing orgasms.

His hard chest caught me as I draped over him, him still inside me. My heart warmed at the kiss on my forehead while I rose and fell with the movement of his chest. I listened to his heartbeat calm as I played with the spattering of curly black hair along his broad chest. Clay still stuck to him in places, and our peaceful evening brought a smile to my face.

"You still got some clay," I whispered between giggles.

"Ow! Hey!" Reid feigned hurt as I picked off the dry bits. "Watch the chest hair. Also, I'm pretty sure I saw some ice cream smeared on your stomach," he laughed.

Grabbing his hand, I led him to the shower where we took turns washing off each other's bodies.

twenty-six

reid

THIS WAS RIGHT.

Daisy's head was on my chest. My arm was wrapped around her. Her leg was draped over me.

If things weren't so perfect right now, I might've be mad at myself for not allowing this to happen sooner.

"Want to call out tomorrow and spend the day in bed?" I asked, stroking lazy circles on her arm.

The moment couldn't have been any more perfect, and her laughter only added to its beauty. "I'm a small business owner. There is no calling out."

"What about your new gal?"

"Polly?"

"Yeah, you said she's been keen on saving up—maybe she'll want some extra hours?" Gripping her perfect, tight ass, I rolled her on top of me. Lightly, I trailed my fingertips along her spine and knew I was winning when she hummed against my chest.

"You make a compelling argument," she said, her voice muffled. "Fine, I'll text Polly first thing in the morning...I can hear your smirk," she deadpanned.

"I'm not smirking," I lied.

"Liar."

A few moments passed and I held my breath, deciding if I should bring up something that had been plaguing my mind. Across her incredibly perfect and sexy leg laid a lengthy scar, indicative of a serious accident. I wasn't sure what we were or where this was going, but my chest ached at the secret she held there.

I decided to wait, trusting she would share with me when she was ready. As freewheeling and honest Daisy was, I also noticed she was secretive. I could feel there was darkness she was trying to hide, maybe forget. The whole Carl debacle was just the tip of the iceberg.

Instead, I wanted to focus on what was happening in the moment. Between us.

"I don't do boyfriends," Daisy blurted, her head now propped in her hands. My eyebrows furrowed. Taking the cue to explain, she continued. "For a long time, I've been the only person I could depend on, rely on. I've been on my own since I turned eighteen and even then, I was already pretty much the only one caring for myself. I promised myself I'd never put myself in a position again to depend on someone."

Keeping my composure, I continued scratching my hands along her back. Her confession made me want to squeeze her and never let go, so I kept my hands busy.

"What about Kendrick?" I asked.

"He wasn't my boyfriend. We were just dating. Hanging out, really. We never had a talk of any sorts, other than when I cut things off with him."

"Did you have this 'I don't do boyfriends' talk with him as well?"

"I—I didn't. I guess things just feel a little different with you and I wanted to be honest."

My heart skipped as she spoke, and I tried not to feel smug. "I appreciate that. And if it's my turn to be honest, I rarely do relationships either. But I don't know. I think things feel different with you, too."

"Why don't you do relationships?"

"Relationships are messy. People get hurt. In a world with billions of people, I am the only person I can control—except when it comes to you. When you're in the picture I apparently lose all my composure. You drive me fucking wild." I tickled her side and smiled at her giggles. "Giving someone else power terrifies me. I struggled with having any say over my own life for so long. I don't want to give someone else the chance to take that away again."

"So, let's agree then. This," she motioned a finger between us, "is not a relationship."

I bit the side of my cheek; something was holding me back from agreeing. A recent memory popped into my head, and I remembered only weeks ago I was dating someone I didn't even particularly like. Hell, we were going to get engaged. The thought of what almost was made my stomach lurch.

"Whoa, you alright there? You look like you're going to be sick," she said, confusion on her face and concern in her voice.

"I feel like I might be," I sighed. She went to make a move, but I held her in place. "No, stay. I'll be fine. I need to tell you something."

She laid on top of me as I told her about the situation with Liz, my parents and the Dickover's. My palms were wet with anxiety as I admitted my weakness for my family. My palms never sweated and, *wow*, I hated it. The knots in my stomach made me realize how much I cared about what Daisy thought. Her opinions mattered to me. A lot.

"Damn," was all she said in response, and I was worried about what was going through her pretty blonde head. After a silent pause, a slick smile crossed her face. "Is her last name really Dickover? That is unfortunate."

We laughed together and I appreciated her light heartedness. She sighed deeply. "I commend you for wanting to protect your parents. You know the glaring issues with my family. My mom stealing from me and all, and her ex, you know, trashing my business and threatening me. But with all that, I still want to protect my mom, too.

"She tried. At least I like to think she did. When I was little, I used to hate bouncing between her boyfriend's houses. All I needed was my mom, you know? But now, I think it was her way of providing for me. Often times, her boyfriend's houses would be the only place I'd get a full meal. In every new town, she always got a new server or cashier gig. She'd pay bills for a while, take me grocery shopping, but eventually, the alcohol won every time."

Her voice was distant, and I could see the lingering pain in her eyes. She was so strong; she carried herself with kindness and understanding but had the grit to get this far in life on her own. My heart swelled with pride knowing that through that, I was the man she chose to lie with. I continued listening intently as her gaze grew more distant with memory.

"When I look at her, though, I see a broken and lost woman. I've tried so hard to cut contact, but she keeps reeling me back in. When one of her boyfriends landed me in the hospital, I finally had the nerve to walk away for good. I didn't talk to her for years, didn't even tell her where I went. Then one day I noticed my credit score tanked. She had opened a credit card with my information. I had just opened this place. I couldn't afford not to have credit available to me.

"Oh, I was so mad. I tracked her down—it wasn't hard. She was still with Carl. I watched and waited for him to leave for work, then banged on the door like a madwoman. She came out, her arm in a sling. I tried then to help her. I took her to a woman's shelter in Baltimore and gave her a phone so I could check on her every day. A month later, she was back with him.

"I still pay for her phone," she laughed bitterly. "I can't help myself. I'd never forgive myself if something happened to her and she wasn't able to reach me for help."

I loosened the grip I had tightened at the mention of being at the hospital. Taking a steadying breath, I calmed myself down, trying not to take away from her deep confession.

"You were just a child, Daisy. It was not your responsibility. And even now, as an adult, you are still her child. It is not your responsibility." I said, steadily.

"I know," she sighed. "But the same could be said for you. You're the child in your situation. It is not your responsibility to make sure your parents' secrets stay secrets."

I stayed silent. She was right. Of course, she was right. I figured as much out myself, but that didn't change the fact that I still went along with it at first.

"You mentioned being in the hospital," my voice cracked. Emotions got the best of me, and I couldn't stop myself from asking. "Is that where that scar on your leg is from?" She closed her eyes and nodded. "Will you tell me?" I asked softly, stroking her hair.

"Carl," her voice wavered. Clearing her throat, she continued. "Carl has always been a real son of a bitch." I let loose a deep belly laugh. I reveled in the way she always found humor in the toughest of times.

"Carl had picked up me and my mom up from the park. We had walked there with a few sandwiches and chips and had a small picnic. I was a week away from graduation and we daydreamed about what I would do, where I would go, who I would be. When she wasn't drinking, she was my best friend. It's like the two sides of her, the sober side and drunk side, didn't even know the other existed. We would laugh and joke and dream about me making it as a big fashion designer or author or what have you. Then she'd come home drunk and beg me not to leave. Plead for me to stay."

The lump in my throat grew. Playing with her hair, I kept myself tethered to reality. I kept myself present for her and pushed away the urge to burn the world for her.

"Sober her wanted me to find a way out. Drunk her couldn't let me go. Neither of her personalities knew I was planning to leave the day after receiving my diploma.

"Anyhow, we weren't at the house when Carl got home from work and, for some reason, that threw him into a rage. He drove around town looking for us. His buddy at the corner store said we had stopped in for bags of chips and instantly he knew where we had gone.

"He yanked us both by the arms and shoved us in his car. He was swerving all over the road because he was too busy putting his attention on my mom. His fist flew like one of those rock em' sock em' robots. You know, like when a kid keeps pushing the trigger. He was hitting her, calling her a whore, a bum. I yelled at him to stop. I was begging and crying, but nothing would stop him."

Her eyes watered, and I restrained myself from scooping her into me. The anger that had taken over grew impossibly bigger. I held steady, stroking her hair and gave her space to continue.

"I'll never forget the look in his eyes," she continued, sniffling briefly. "He turned to me and his eyes were nearly black. He said, 'I'll put you in a coma, you ungrateful bitch.' That was the last thing I remembered. Two weeks later, I woke up in the hospital, my leg bandaged. I was covered in cuts and scrapes, and I even had trouble seeing out of one eye for a few weeks. I still get migraines sometimes. They say they'll likely never go away.

"The sheriff came in when he heard I had woken up. Apparently, while Carl was too distracted hitting my mom, he swerved into oncoming traffic. He over corrected, and we tail span into a pole. It hit right on the back passenger door. The door ripped and the metal came inward, slicing my leg open. The sheriff said if we'd been going any faster, I likely would've died. The cut was an inch away from my femoral artery. I don't remember the exact terminology, but had that been cut, it would have been no bueno.

"But like Tina Turner, I will survive, you know? Missed my prom, graduation, and birthday, but hell. I was finally free."

Words escaped me and instead I brought my hands to hold her face and pulled her to me, our lips meeting softly. My heart tugged at the feeling that took over when our lips touched. I hung on a moment longer, deepening our kiss.

With her face still in my hands, our eyes connected, I took in the wild, proud, strong woman in front of me. "I am so sorry you went through that alone, Daisy."

Tears brimmed at her lash line, and she nodded silently, kissing me again.

"So, tell me more about high-school-Daisy. I bet you were a total bad ass. Or wait...Daisy Bloom, were you a cheerleader?" I asked, another hour and life altering orgasm later. I meant it when I said I couldn't get enough of her.

"A cheerleader?" she snorted. "Nah, though I did try out at my second high school. I hoped it would help me fit in, but it did the opposite when I accidentally farted while trying to do a herkie."

It was my turn to snort, and she slapped me on the chest.

"Farting is a bodily function! Nothing to be embarrassed about," she exclaimed, turning a shade of pink that made me smile so hard my cheeks started hurting. "I never really stuck around long enough to make friends, so I was willing to try pretty much anything."

"No boyfriends either?"

"I wished." She rolled her eyes heavily. "My only boyfriend was a picture of Nick Jonas I taped to the inside of my notebook. Ripped the cover of a Tiger Beat magazine off in a store one day, and it stayed in my notebook all year. Anytime a boy wouldn't give me the time of day, I'd just flip open my notebook, blow a kiss to Nicky-poo, and feel all better about myself."

I feigned shock. "You shoplifting rebel."

"Hey, the teen years weren't easy ones, Flores. There was this one boy, though, that I had a major crush on. Never learned his name, but he had this funny nickname his friends gave him because he looked just like his pet iguana."

"Iggy," we said at the same time, mine as more of a question.

My high school nickname on her lips brought back a flood of memories.

The blonde girl with a blue streak who popped up one day a few months before graduation. I invited her to join me and my friends for lunch on her first day, but she rarely joined us after that. The minute she walked through Mrs. Larkin's room, her blue eyelashes matching her blue highlights perfectly, I was done in. Many long showers were dedicated to my wild-haired teenage dream girl.

I was going to ask her as my date to prom, but a week before, she vanished. Eventually, I convinced myself I must've made her up. In my memories her name had been Lily, Rose, Hazel, Violet, but never Daisy. Why didn't I ever remember her name was Daisy?

Recognition clicked as we stared into each other's eyes, dissecting the years we'd missed hidden behind our age.

"Iggy?" she asked, bewildered.

"Super cool blue-haired dream girl?" I asked, just as dazed. A light smile played at her lips at the nickname. "I can't believe this. What happened? Where did you go?"

"Ha," she laughed, "the car crash and coma, remember?"

"Yeah, but..." there really was no *but* about it, I knew that. Still, my chest ached at the disappointment I felt all those years ago. Blowing out a breath, I pushed my fingers through my hair. "You know, I was going to ask you to prom."

Shooting to an upright position, she covered her mouth with her hand. "No," she gasped.

"Yes. Very much, yes. I learned to bake that weekend, I guess the weekend of your accident. I made my first ever cake from scratch and planned on bringing it to school on Monday. A double chocolate cake, and I used silver edible glitter to write PROM? on the top. My aunt helped me make it look legible. I was so nervous my letters came out all shaky."

"That is fucking adorable," she laughed, her eyes watering with emotion. "Oh, Reid, I would have died if you did that. Thank you so much."

"Well, consider this a full circle moment. You got to try my world-famous peach cobbler." I tried not being smug, but the way she looked at me now, the gratitude in her eyes, I felt like the king of the world. "After baking your cake, I realized I actually enjoyed baking. My Aunt and I would try new recipes every weekend. That peach cobbler was the second recipe we learned."

"Does your aunt live here? It sounds like you two are close."

"We are, but she lives back in Maryland. My parents shipped me off to live with her for high school so I could realize everything they provided for me. It was their way of manipulating me into going into business and finance."

"That's why you were in Maryland? Because your parents used it as punishment?"

"Yeah," I sighed. "I signed up for the STEM curriculum, instead of the business curriculum, without their approval. When my freshmen year schedule came in and they realized what I had done, they said I didn't appreciate the life they'd given me. Aunt Suzy was middle-class, nowhere near poverty, yet she was far enough away from rich that they saw it as punishment. So, off to Maryland with Aunt Suzy I went. I ended up loving my time there. Aunt Suzy is kind, supportive, and learned to bake with me. All moving me there did was hurt my relationship with my parents."

"And, now, here you are."

"Here I am. I moved back the summer before college, then moved out of my parent's house the day I signed my full-time job offer. I still talk to my Aunt Suzy almost daily."

"Does she know about the whole 'marry Liz so no one finds out I'm a cheating asshole' thing? Sorry, no offense meant."

Chuckling, I shook my head. "No offense taken. And no, she doesn't. She would just get in a fight with my mom about it...but she knows about you."

"Moi?" She placed a hand to chest and flipped her hair playfully.

"Yeah. She knows you're a feisty, sexy pain in my ass."

"Aren't you lucky?" She winked at me, and she really had no idea just how lucky I was.

"I sure am." I pulled her back into me. "So, how did *you* get here?"

"Well, at the time of the accident, I had finished all my classes, except one. But, thankfully, Mrs. Larkin let me take my final exam after I woke up."

"Mrs. Larkin? Mrs. I-eat-chalk-and-steal-children's-souls-Larkin?"

I could feel her smile against me as she shook her head. "Turns out Mrs. Larkin was actually Mrs. I-am-a-survivor-and-help-other-sur-vivors-and-keep-a-hard-exterior-as-a-defense-mechanism-Larkin. I confided in her about the accident, and about Carl. She shared her own story and told me to come back the next day. When I did, she handed me a card with five hundred dollars in it to send me on my way."

Staring at the ceiling, I laid flabbergasted.

"The card is framed and is hanging in the living room," she contin-ued. "It's a watercolor painting of a small town. The sun is setting, and families are walking the streets. It's serene. Nothing bad ever happens there. I hung it up to remind me of the good people do in the world, and that peaceful places exist, just like in the picture. Because of the money she gave me, I was able to get a bus ticket out of town. I rode until I found this place—just like the painting on the card. The rest of the money was just enough to pay for the first month's rent for a room in a house I shared with six other people. Then I found a job at Loop & Scoop, and here I am."

Her incredible strength continued to amaze me. She could be any-where in the world—sailing across oceans, selling art in Italy, designing clothes in Paris, but she chose to make peace here. Hope bloomed in me at what peace we could build together.

I kissed her deeply, rolling her further into the sheets.

"Here you are."

twenty-seven

daisy

"LISTEN HERE, BUCKAROO, YOU better stop calling here and harassing my dear Daisy. You're wanted for property damage and breaking and entering by-" Polly threatened through the phone before slamming it back on the receiver. "The schmuck has some nerve calling here after what he did."

"Carl, again?" I asked, exasperated. Didn't he have anything better to do? He'd gotten his rocks off breaking nearly every piece of pottery in my shop. What more did calling here accomplish?

The Birchwood shelves Marley and Reid fixed were stunning. Their pale honeyed color was gorgeous, and perfect at warming up the space with an equally calming quality. The muted beauty sat backseat, letting the art speak for itself. However, I wouldn't be me if I didn't add a pop of color to the space. With a utility knife in my mouth, I worked to apply wallpaper adorned with pink tinted jungle animals on the wall space between the shelf cubbies.

"Yeah," Polly sighed, scratching her head. "I'll add the number to the list for Rick to block."

Polly's techy contact at the shelter, Rick, had already blocked seven numbers and counting. Last I remembered, Carl barely had enough money to keep instant ramen on the shelf of his dilapidated condo. How on earth was he able to afford to get a new number every day?

"So, uh, how was your day off yesterday?" Polly asked, pretending to be super interested in the pottery sale tag she was filling out.

Wanting to give nothing away, I shrugged. "Fine."

"Mmhmm," she hummed in a questioning tone. "If I spent the day in bed with my own personal sex god, my day would be better than fine." Before I could ask her how she knew, she continued. "*Please*. The way that man looks at you..." she fanned herself. "Phew! And I couldn't help but notice that neither of you came down yesterday."

Staring ahead, I tilted my head, assessing the pink painted jaguar. And dammit, it felt like that feline queen was judging me. Not very "queens straighten other queens crowns" of her. Alas, it meant the jaguar knew. Polly knew. And hell, that meant half of Chestnut Hills knew too.

With a groan, I gently knocked my forehead into the shelf in front of me.

"Should I take that as the sex not being good?" Polly quipped behind me.

"It was better than good," I murmured into the wood. Lifting my head, I turned to face her, "but I'm not going to talk about it. Because there is no 'it.' There is nothing to talk about. Not a thing—that's what nothing means, you know?"

"Right. Okay. Forget I mentioned it."

"So, you ready for your first First Fridays?" I asked, changing the subject.

"You bet'cha. Poppy is going to stop by too! I can't wait to show her our setup," Polly said, glowing as she spoke about her daughter.

"I can't wait to meet her."

The First Fridays was even busier than the last. The street was filled fifteen minutes into kick-off, and the Assets were set to close out the evening in an hour. Being that the Assets were a local celebrity band and had never played First Fridays before, this was a big deal.

I had to see the set. Reid was already one hell of a man, but when he played the drums? It was like tunnel vision took over. All I could see was him.

Polly agreed to man the booth so I could sneak off to watch their set. She was more than happy to trade off when I shooed her away to spend some time with her copy and paste look-a-like daughter. Glowing and sharing a pretzel with Poppy, Polly glided back to the booth, grinning like a fiend.

"Thanks Daisy," Polly said quietly, giving my arm a squeeze. "You have no idea what that meant to me." My heart ached for what they had. Knowing that I had it in my own way at one point heightened the pain. I gave Polly a wink in return and left it at that, pushing my hurt away.

"Hello gorgeous," a deep, sultry voice called behind me.

A golden glow from the setting sun spotlit Reid, and my tummy did a little flippity flop thing. I smiled at him as he approached and soaked in his confidence and swagger.

A small woman came around him, walking by his side. His height made her look tinier, but she was probably just as tall as me. Her stark black hair was blown out in waves, and her make-up was applied light and pristine. She held her head high as she walked. Her designer bag dangled at one elbow while her other hand clutched a brown paper bag.

"Daisy, this is my mom, Carrey Flores," he said as he approached, putting his arm around his mom.

"Pleasure," I said with a smile and extended my hand. "Daisy Bloom, owner of Slay & Clay."

Carrey appraised me from head to toe, taking in my green lacey layered dress and pink streaked hair. "Nice to meet you, Daisy," she said, pursing her lips.

Making small talk, Reid told me how much they were enjoying the market—Carrey's first one. It was an even more special night because Carrey was going to watch her son play the drums for the first time. At Reid's urging to talk, his mom asked to learn more about my pottery classes. I explained to her my program and class levels while Reid's eyes seared through me.

Knowing I was under his gaze, my skin prickled. Even more overcoming, my panties nearly set ablaze when he winked at me as a way of goodbye.

"Your day was just 'fine,' my ass," Polly said under her breath behind me. "Nothing about that man is 'just fine.'"

The crowd around the stage was growing. Folding chairs and blankets littered the lawn as people chowed down on vendor hot dogs, popcorn, and cotton candy. Brian and Louis were on stage, setting all the instruments up. Kara's electric red hair flashed on the side of the stage as she chatted with a woman in a leather vest. A figure moved behind a tall set of speakers, and I knew from the height it must be Reid.

After the eye foreplay earlier, nothing would have made me happier than a kiss from my hunky not-boyfriend.

Reid's hushed voice traveled from behind the speaker. "Thanks for coming to see me play tonight, mom. It means a lot to me," he said. I paused, wanting to give them space to have this conversation.

"Of course, son. Thank you for this evening. It has been a joy to experience the market, and I cannot wait for your showcase," his mom replied. Though she seemed to be a stoic, proper woman—must be where Reid got it—I could hear the excitement hiding in her voice.

"Concert, mom," he said flatly.

"Concert, yes. I will likely leave before it ends, if that's alright with you." There was a brief pause before she continued. "I have to ask, before you go, the pottery girl-"

"Daisy?"

"Yes, Daisy. Well, I just...please do not tell me you broke things off for Liz for that *artist*." The disgust that tinged her voice made me recoil.

"I broke things off with Liz for me. We talked about this. I was unhappy. Daisy makes me happy, so I am pursuing things with Daisy. You said you wanted this for me, for me to be happy."

"I did. I do. I just meant with someone of more...standing."

"Standing?" he asked, bewildered.

"Yes, Reid. You know. Someone who comes from the same background as us. Someone who knows the difference between a soup spoon and dessert spoon. Not someone who puts pink in her hair and wears a dirty apron while struggling to pay the bills."

Heat crept into my cheeks at her words. The heat, I quickly recognized, was searing anger. Not shame. Nothing could make me feel ashamed of the success I've made for myself.

"Whoa, whoa, let's back up a moment," Reid started, and he sounded mad. So mad, in fact, that I decided to hold my anger back and not march right around the speaker and give Carrey a piece of my mind.

"I can't even process the wild and incorrect assumptions you threw in there. She isn't struggling to pay the bills, she's ridiculously successful and runs a small business with employees. That's *multiple* employees. Her apron isn't dirty, it's the product of her creating art.

And she puts pink in her hair because she is true to herself, something we both have admitted we could try harder at."

My heart swelled at being not only appreciated, but also seen.

"That may be all true, Reid, but-"

"But nothing, mom. End of discussion. Drive home safe and enjoy the show," Reid interrupted and huffed. Carrey must have stormed off because she came around the speaker, hot; she didn't even see me on the other side.

Reid was walking to the stage stairs with a little slump in his shoulders. I called after him, jogging lightly to catch up to him. His expression instantly brightened at seeing me, but I caught the sadness that flashed. Before he could speak, I threw my arms around his neck and planted a kiss on his lips.

Our surroundings quieted and slowed as our lips met and opened to each other. He tasted like cinnamon and sweet cream; he smelled like wood and ember, something I decided I would remember forever. Finally, I pulled our faces apart.

"Have a great show. I'll be watching." I winked and twirled out of his grip. With a wave, I disappeared around the corner and took my faithful spot right in front.

twenty-eight

reid

"Okay, if aliens invaded Earth and gave you the option to stay here or return to space with them, what would you choose?" Daisy asked between sips of coffee.

I took a contemplative bite out of an apple. "That depends. Are they friendly?"

"You don't know yet."

"Well, what if they want to whisk me away to impregnate me and reproduce their species?"

"Impregnate?" she spat out her coffee. "That'd be impossible."

"They're aliens. Anything is possible," I shrugged. "Could I bring you?"

"No."

"Then hard pass. If you're staying, I'm staying," I winked. Light pink tinged her cheeks, and she eyed me over her coffee mug.

The weeks had come and gone, and the calls from Carl still came like clockwork. Luckily, there were no more break-ins. For now. And as much as I had hate brewing in my gut for Carl, I appreciated his stubbornness, because it gave me reason to stay with Daisy longer.

Things felt good. Lightness filled my movements in a way it hadn't before, and I was happy. The air mattress was deflated and packed away, and I was the proud receiver, and giver, of nearly daily orgasms. Lucky me.

"Listen," Daisy chippered, "I have this thing I'm going to next weekend. Don't read into it or anything, but you're welcome to join."

"Do you want me to come?" I asked.

"Only if you want," she hedged.

"That's not what I asked. I want you to tell me that you want me to come."

"Reid, I want you to come."

"Done. I'll be there." I hid my fiendish smile that threatened to break. We may have agreed to not label what was going on between us, but we were essentially in a committed relationship. A year ago, that would have sent my balls straight up into my stomach and my ass right onto the floor. But with Daisy, I wanted it. All.

She, however, I thought still needed a little convincing. I was trying my best not to spook the horse, so to speak.

"You don't even know what it is."

"And I don't need to. Whatever it is, if you want me there, I'm there." Hell, I thought, it could be a butter churning convention and I'd still want to go if Daisy was there.

"It's the National Pottery and Ceramics Showcase," she said, tucking a stray hair behind her ear. "I've always wanted to go—it's like a hall of fame for contemporary pottery and ceramics makers. It's for two days in New York City."

The excitement in her words was adorable. Her grin was wide as she giggled sweetly, and though I couldn't see her feet, I imagined they were kicking back and forth under the table. Giddy like a kid counting down the days until summer break, her excitement was contagious.

"Sounds like a blast," I smiled. "Are you able to enter your own work? You should bring *Dark Parts Bloom.*"

Her sculpture had really started taking shape. The glaze needed to dry for another day or two, then she could complete her last fire and be done. The flowers erupting from the chest were beautifully and painstakingly made, with the tiniest details paid attention to. The pollen looked soft and fluffy, as if it would float away if you breathed too hard.

"I wish," she snorted. "It's not a bring your own work kind of thing. These artists are scouted. A few times a year, they host competitions to be entered, but I've always been too nervous to submit my work."

"Why's that? Your stuff is amazing."

"What if they don't like it? I've found purpose in what I do. I don't know if I could handle being told it's not good enough. I've spent enough of my life not being good enough. I'm not looking to go back to that feeling." Her voice quieted as she spoke, trailing down to a whisper.

The Daisy I knew was strong and determined. She laughed in the face of fear and did everything overflowing with courage. I always thought she let her childlike spirit shine, but I realized that was her protecting herself. Because her childlike spirit was abandoned and deeply hurt a long time ago.

That didn't sit right with me. I wanted to rush in on my horse in my shining armor and slay her demons. Instead, I stroked her hand across the table and gave it a squeeze.

"They would be fools to not appreciate your work. And regardless of what anyone thinks of you, you are beyond good enough. You are too good for this world, and I will walk beside you while you figure that out for yourself."

She smiled at that, and my heart just about melted away.

twenty-nine

daisy

"DAZE, PLEASE," REID RESTED his hand on my knee. His other hand lazily held the steering wheel as we whirred up the turnpike. "You're ruining the suspension of my car with all that shaking."

Contrasting his practical personality, Reid drove a sultry green sports car. The angles of the design made it look like we were jetting into the future. The purr under my butt added to the excitement bubbling in my belly.

"Sorry," I said, my finger in my mouth as I chewed at the nail.

"I think I can help you release some of that energy," he chuckled, sliding his hand further up my leg.

Heat coursed through me as his fingers grazed under the hem of my skirt. Taking the hitch of my breath as permission, he kept coasting higher until he reached the apex of my thighs. My inner thighs tingled with his touch, as it did every time he touched me there. The pleasure he gave me was intoxicating. I feared I would never get enough.

On a sigh, I opened my legs to him.

Music murmured through the speakers as the road whirred by and the car vibrated beneath me. Through the cotton, his fingers began creating a sweet friction. I pulled my underwear to the side for him. Slowly, he began circling my clit. Desire racked me and I thrusted into his hand.

Quick with his work, he pushed his finger into me, then two. Methodically, he thrusted his fingers into me, curling them at the right spot. Tension evaporated from my body and I melted into his touch. A moan passed my lips as I threw my head back, closing my eyes. I stilled, my breath turning ragged, as I drank in the bliss he threw my body into. Slowly, I traveled my down to work myself as he thrusted, adding to the euphoria.

"That's right, baby. Make yourself come on my fingers," he demanded, his voice low.

I needed nothing more as my walls contracted around him and my body shook. My back arched off the back of the seat and I cried out in pleasure.

Removing his fingers at glacier speed, additional spasms coursed through me. I watched as he sucked his coated fingers clean. The sight of it, the way he took pleasure in the taste, nearly made me blackout. Righting myself, I readjusted my underwear and sat up straight.

The National Pottery and Ceramics Showcase was grand, taking up an entire floor of conference rooms on the top level of a skyscraper hotel. White pristine drapes cascaded across the rafters and art coated the walls, bringing color to the space. Vendor tables were decorated to fit the ambiance, and stood between displays of pottery, sculptures and ceramics.

My mouth watered with excitement. I was a kid and this was my candy store.

"You're drooling," Reid whispered from behind me.

"Only a little," I said, closing my gaping mouth. "Where do we start?"

"We have all day, baby," he kissed my neck. Lacing his fingers through mine, he guided me to the first vendor table selling handmade pottery trimming tools.

Faithfully, he stood next to me as we walked from table to table. He listened dutifully as experts taught me tips and tricks. He asked questions about other artist's work. He didn't judge when I jumped up and down clapping when they announced Macy Shivers would host a "throw with me" class.

Over dinner in a little ramen shop, he told me how much he admired my passion. He told me how inspiring it was to watch me pursue my dreams. He told me all this while perusing my cleavage with his eyes and wetting his lips.

Unlocking the door to our—what was my—hotel room, he kept his grip on my waist.

"You know, I've been thinking since our first night together," he started, unbuttoning the first few buttons of his shirt. A tuft of chest hair on his sculpted chest peaked through. "You had your fun playing teacher. It's only fair I had the same."

Gliding across the room, he approached me. Brushing my hair out of my face, he kissed up my neck. His fingers dug into my waist as he gripped me with his other hand, and I felt powerless. Yet, the power I lacked here was welcomed. I wanted a break, a chance to fall into someone else. If there was anyone in this world I trusted with this, it was—well, it was actually Ellie—but Reid was second. Definitely second. But Ellie had some serious competition.

"My turn to teach you a few lessons." His fingers slid under the waistband of my skirt and gripped my ass. "On the bed."

Obeying his command, I silently perched myself in the middle of the king-sized bed. Drawing my feet under me, my eyes followed him as he walked around the bed, revealing Velcro cuffs tethered to something from under the mattress.

"I snuck up here during the seminar on clay types," he explained. Moving to the other side of the bed, he pulled out two more cuffs. "They're under the bed restraints. Nothing too serious, but enough to keep you tied up for my pleasure—and yours. Only if you're okay with it," he prompted, opening a cuff.

Silently, I assessed. Reid was a domineering man, and yet he had always made me feel like the one with the power. Ultimately, I trusted him and the heat growing in my core told me I wanted this. Biting my lip, I nodded.

"Sure, okay," I said hesitantly. "I—I've never done anything like this, though."

"I'll be gentle," he said with a wink. "If anything, let's come up with a word. You say this word the minute you want out, and I'll untie you immediately. No questions asked."

"Sprinkles?"

"Okay," he smiled warmly. "You say 'sprinkles,' and we immediately stop."

His kindness and affirmation felt good. This felt good. Excitement coursed through me, and my body vibrated with anticipation.

Moving across the bed, he sat in front of me and lifted my shirt off, revealing my black cotton bra. Pausing a moment, he looked me over and kissed the middle of my chest gently. Guiding me to lie down, he fasted a cuff on each hand, pulling them above my head.

I began squirming as he trailed his tongue down the center of my body. Landing at the waist of my skirt, he tugged at it, pulling it down just an inch. His tongue explored along my hips, and I lifted to meet him.

"Tsk, tsk," he scolded softly. "Lesson one, patience is rewarded. Greed is not." He moved to cuff my ankles at the opposite corners of the bed, making sure to graze his lips along my large scar.

Never had I been on display in such a powerless position. As my heart raced and my palms grew damp with sweat, I felt a wave of vulnerability wash over me. Every inch of my body seemed to tremble with a mix of fear, helplessness, and fiery lust. My usual confident demeanor had evaporated, leaving me exposed; and I chose to lean into it.

With each breath coming in rushed pants, I eagerly awaited his next move. At the foot of the bed, he stood, his hands on his hips, his cock straining against his zipper. Gruffly, he rubbed his face.

"You're so gorgeous, baby. I could stare at you all day like this," he said, his eyes heavy. Lightly, he brushed his fingers along my leg, from my ankle, up my thigh. He grazed across my mound and trailed down the other leg.

Crawling up the bed, he positioned himself between my legs, his face at the nape of my neck. Then the assault began—his lips crushed against my sensitive skin, and he sucked, licked, nipped, and kissed. Across my collarbone and up to each ear, he didn't miss an inch. I tilted my head to give him more access as he moved around me. In a state of pleasure, my back involuntarily arched off the bed.

His hands roamed my body. Exploring my midsection, he teased my breasts, thumbing beneath the band of my bra. I ached to touch him, to run my hands along the muscles of his back, to kiss him in the same places he kissed me. The restraints tugged as I pulled against them. Wetness grew at my core at the eroticism of it all. Never had I been so consumed.

"Let's see those gorgeous tits," he said, unclasping the front of my bra in a swift motion.

Determination coated his face, and he greedily took a nipple into his mouth while palming the other. Working between the two, he mimicked the kissing, sucking, licking, and biting he had rained on my neck.

"Reid," I said on a breath, "you make me feel so good."

Attentive to not leave a spot unmarked, he took his time down my body. His beard brushed along my bare skin as his lips skimmed me, leaving embers in his wake of where he'd set on fire. Moving across my navel, he gently bit at my waist. *Holy shit.*

With a gentle motion, he lifted my skirt and delicately brushed his lips over the soft cotton fabric that was covering my sensitive flesh. His breath tickled me in a way that made me pulse, nearly bringing me to satisfaction. "Oh god Reid," I cried, not wanting to admit how embarrassingly close I was already.

"So responsive," he said, repeating the motion. "I haven't even feasted yet." He sucked me roughly, the cotton acting as a barrier. I cursed the defiant fabric, wanting to feel his lips there too. Lacking the immediate satisfaction that would provide, my anticipation of release built. The teasing and excitement of what was inevitably going to come next brought satisfaction surging through me and waves rocked my body.

Teasing me through my underwear, my body rode the last waves of pleasure, only to be brought right back to the brink.

Attention shifting, he gave a resounding slap to my inner thigh. I gasped in surprise, the sting of pain overtaken by the crave it created. Gripping the band of my underwear, Reid gave a swift tug, ripping the fabric straight through. Discarding it, he looked at me hungrily.

"That's much better," he said with a sinister smile. I couldn't even rub two brain cells together to be upset about the torn underwear.

Spreading my slit with his hands, he flicked my clitoris with the tip of his tongue. A scream slipped past my lips and, just like that, I was on the brink of freefall again. Driven with purpose, Reid dove in. Lapping me up, he worked my sensitive nub with ferocity.

One hand filled me with one finger, then two, then three, methodically adding a finger every few thrusts. The other pinched and tugged at a nipple. I was being played with, pulled, and praised all at once. I couldn't bear it. I thought I might explode.

"That's it, baby. Grip my fingers with your pussy," he lovingly guided me. I squeezed my walls around him, beckoning my orgasm to come quicker. "I can feel you, Daisy. You're right there. Come on my face."

With that, I lost all control. Spasms wracked my body as I shook against the restraints. He dutifully licked every drop as I coated his face and fingers. Pulling away, he gave my swollen and sensitive flesh a sharp slap. The additional attention made my body jolt once more.

With a satisfied grin on his face, he removed the cuffs with care. I watched him with his cheshire grin as I took steadying breaths, attempting to recover from the frenzy. Without effort, he lifted me to his chest and carried me to the large and luxurious shower. Setting me on the tiled seat, he began running the water.

Together we showered. Taking care to lather each other as if we were the others' only prized possession.

Something funny tickled my gut as I looked at the man before me. I'd never needed someone before, but the way I was beginning to feel...I feared my independence may be challenged. This man didn't give me life, but he supported me to continue to build mine. He didn't pay my bills or grant me security, but he did stand next to me as I pursued my passions and cheered me on without fail.

My heart swelled with content. I was at peace.

thirty
reid

"How goes it, son?" my dad asked, his fork full of lettuce and chicken. My parents invited me for a late afternoon lunch. Since most of my free time lately had been consumed by Daisy, I hadn't seen my dad in weeks. I was still spending time with mom, and that was what really mattered, anyhow. The more I thought things over, the more I looked at the situation from every angle, the more I couldn't stand the thought of seeing my dad.

Daisy was a welcome reprieve from the stress of that part of my life. The days felt easy with her. I'd return to her apartment after work and cook her dinner. We'd watch a show or two on nights she wasn't closing shop. Then we'd fall asleep, her wrapped in my arms. There was still no defining us. At first, I was okay with that, but as time went on, the more I wanted the label. I wanted to be hers, and I wanted her to declare she was mine.

"Good," I responded, contemplating if I should bring up Daisy. "I've been seeing someone."

Looking at me over his salad, my dad's eyebrows rose so high that they blended with his hairline. Mom busied herself, sipping her water and pushing around her chicken.

"So, I've heard," Clinton sighed. My parents made eye contact, having themselves a silent conversation. One I'd seen before. I knew something was coming. "I wanted to talk to you about that. Your mother explained to you our predicament, and I had expected you to do the honorable thing—for your family."

"Well, I could say the same for you," I said in a questioning tone. Mom gasped my name under her breath, unhappy with my bringing up the topic.

Red crept into dad's face, and he gripped his fork. "Son, this is not a discussion. You will break things off with the artist girl and resume your relationship with Elizabeth."

Casually wiping my mouth, I stood. Looking my father in the eyes, I was calm. "I will do no such thing, dad. I love Daisy. Your sins are not mine to pay."

Had I really said that? I said such without thinking, but it was true. I wasn't sure when it happened. Maybe it happened when I first stumbled on her broken-into shop and her only concern was about paying her clients on time. Maybe it was when I learned one of her missions was to provide opportunities to people in recovery. Maybe it was when I watched her twirling around without a care for the first time.

I was in love with Daisy.

Disappointment overwhelmed my senses, surprising me. I wasn't a fan of my parents. Especially not my dad, and even more so after what had just happened. My disdain thrived the more I thought about how they'd tried to control my entire life. They had the authority to ship me off for high school, but now with something as serious as marriage? Well, I was about done.

On the way home—to Daisys. On the way to Daisy's, I stopped at my apartment. I'd been ignoring my responsibilities, choosing to stay in Daisy's bed instead. But I had mail to go through, and clothes to grab.

A sweet smell carried down the hall, and there was no way that was coming from my apartment. Opening the front door, I was smacked by the scent of freshly baked pie.

"Oh shit, man," Chuckie chuckled from the couch. "Been a while."

"Yeah, sorry. Needed to grab my mail. Am I interrupting?" I asked, looking at the oven.

"Nah, Wendy is taking a shower. Should be out any minute."

"Chuckie?" a light voice called from my roommate's room. "Who're you talking to?" A small red head, nearly half Chuckie's size, stepped into the living room in overalls and a shirt. Bent to the side at her waist, she was patting at her still damp hair with a towel.

"Babe, this is Reid. My roommate," Chuckie made introductions from the couch.

Wendy offered me a slice of warm apple pie and vanilla ice cream—I couldn't say no. I listened intently as she told me about her move to Chestnut Hills, and I watched Chuckie's dopey smile.

Damn, if I didn't want that.

Maybe it'd been true—why I didn't do relationships. They had always scared the shit out of me. Daisy scared the shit out of me. But it was the kind of scared I wanted to dive headfirst into. It was the kind of scared that made me want to pick up a torch and venture in with the prospect of returning victorious.

"You missed one, Reid," Wendy said, thumbing through the metal hanging basket with the word MAIL on the front. "Oh, it's a fancy one."

I grabbed the ornate envelope. The deep red of the paper contrasted the bright white ink, conveying the warmth and elegance of the fall season. The return address was precisely written—Clinton and Carrey Flores. No doubt my mom had paid a calligrapher to handwrite all the addresses.

Already knowing what it was, I sighed as I carefully opened the envelope.

Every year, my parents hosted a fall celebration. They called it a "fall celebration," but really it was for my mom to set the standard for parties before the holidays kicked off; and an opportunity for my dad to schmooze the other board members. A small tear through the thick layers of envelope and invitation had just started to grow when Wendy spoke up.

"What are you doing?" she asked, staring at my hands with confusion.

"It's an invitation to my parents' fall celebration. I'm not going," I said.

Chuckie made an *O* with his mouth, understanding the meaning. Over a second slice of pie, Chuckie and I told Wendy of my woman woos from the last few months. She let out a low whistle and looked over the invitation for the third time.

"What if you took Daisy to this thing?" she asked.

I hadn't thought of that, but I could. I should. I wanted to. Was there any better way to show my family my true intention than to bring Daisy?

Before doing that, though, I had to talk to Daisy. She had to know the depth of my feelings for her and that maybe something more serious didn't sound so crazy after all.

Slay & Clay was bustling. The sound of children's laughter and parents' chatter rang about as I approached the propped open front door. Daisy was hosting an open house with pottery painting for the kids. It was her way of making art accessible to all while using the power of kids' sad eyes to guilt parents into buying class packages, then toting the wine paint nights as a great date spot, or parent's night out.

A boy with a stream of snot running from his nose was galloping around screaming and almost collided with my legs. When he came to a halt, a girl with lopsided pigtails and a blue sticky face crashed into his back, sending them both to the ground. Stepping over them, I scanned the chaos for my girl.

Looking over a pot shaped to look like a dog's head, I spotted a head of blonde and pink. Waiting off to the side, I admired her as she worked. She flitted about the space, crouching down to the kid's level, and standing to speak with the adults. Passion sparked in her eyes. Joy radiated off of her.

"Hey hot stuff," she said, approaching and placing a kiss on my lips. I reveled in the taste of sugar and smell of lavender.

"Hey there gorgeous." I felt the inevitable smile that always seemed to find my face when I was around her grow. "Can I steal you away for fifteen minutes?"

Over her shoulder, Polly approached with a light skip. "Reid! Fancy seeing you here," she winked at me. "Hey boss, I got this if you want to take a break. Calley just clocked in. We can hold down the fort."

Calculating the scene, Daisy chewed her lip. "Okay, give me fifteen?" she asked.

"How about thirty?" Polly countered. I mouthed 'thank-you' to her and she gave me a nod and another wink.

The silence and calm of the apartment starkly contrasted the overwhelming mayhem downstairs. Once the door closed, we were in our own world. I swooped her into my arms and crashed my lips to hers, coaxing her into a passionate kiss. Our lips collided as our mouths danced with each other.

A light thud came from behind her as I pushed her into the door and pressed my body against hers. My hands roamed under her shirt, grazing the underside of her breasts. She jumped to wrap her legs around my waist. Gripping my hands under her ass, I carried her to the bedroom.

Her hair fanned around her as she laid on the bed. She was a fairy goddess. With rosy cheeks and pink lips from my assault on her mouth, she looked absolutely delectable. My hands framed her face as I hovered over her. Her hands roamed my chest under my shirt and I kissed her lightly on her nose.

The giggle she released acted like a lasso and grabbed hold of my heart.

"Daisy, I—" I started, wondering if I should let the words that threatened to fall make the jump. "I love you," I whispered.

She loosened a small gasp and moved her hands to my hair. Threading her fingers, she caressed the back of my head and pulled me into a slow, sensual kiss.

"Duh."

"Duh?"

"Of course you love me. I'm amazing," she said with a confident smile.

Chuckling, I shook my head. "You're more than that. You're kind, beautiful, smart, and talented. There's one other thing I want you to be...mine."

"I—I thought, I thought we weren't going to label this."

"We weren't. But now I'd like to. I love you, Daisy. I'm in love with you, and I want this to be real."

"Silly billy, this is real." She pinched my side with a giggle. Grabbing her hand, I pinned it above her head to hold her in place.

"I'm serious, Daisy. You can make jokes, but—look at me." I waited for her eyes to lock on mine. "You can make jokes, but I'm being serious."

Emotion flickered behind her eyes. "The way I feel about you, Reid...it scares me."

"It scares me too," I admitted. "But not having you, this, in my life, scares me more. I need to know now, is this what you want? Because if not, I need to walk away before I fall even harder." A moment passed, and neither of us moved. "I want to hear you say it. The words."

She chewed on her lips, keeping them sealed. It was like her body wouldn't let the words enter the ether.

"Tell me, baby," I said softly, "tell me how you feel." I released her hand above her head as she made a move to frame my face. She looked deep into my soul, and I knew there would be no coming back if she said what I thought, hoped, she was going to say.

"I love you too, Reid," she whispered back.

My strong, confident, independent woman transformed in front of me. Her vulnerability shook me. She was trusting me not to hurt her, and I made a promise to myself I'd do everything in my power to keep her happy and safe.

Peppering kisses around her face, I repeated my infatuation several times.

The flame that was kindled between us grew into an inferno. Passion took over as our kisses deepened, but our confessions kept us in a place of softness. Slowly, we removed each other's clothes. With intentional movements, we savored every spot our skin connected.

She reached down between us, taking my hardened cock into her hand and giving me long, powerful tugs.

"I need you, Reid," she said with desperation. I yanked open the nightstand, searching for a condom. Her hand on my chest stopped me. "I want you, bare. I want to feel you. I need *all* of you."

The thought made me lightheaded. "Are you sure? I've never..."

"Me either," she blushed, "but I want to. With you." Lining me up with her entrance, my breath hitched at the warmth. Slowly, I thrusted into her. Her arousal coated me as I sheathed myself entirely in her and it was pure bliss. As her walls gripped me, I struggled to maintain composure.

"You were fucking made for me, baby," I panted between thrusts. "The way you grip me is pure sin."

She shuddered and moaned my name. The way she called for me, the way my name rolled off her tongue, was an aphrodisiac. If I wasn't already a goner, I was now.

My pace quickened. Our kisses deepened. She bit my shoulder while bringing her hips up to meet mine. The quivering of her walls brought me closer to the edge. Pressure built at the base of my spine and I released just as she tightened around me. Together we experienced unmatchable pleasure as we held each other close and I filled her with each pulse.

We laid in bed after cleaning up, and I twirled a pink strand of hair around my finger. I watched as her breath steadied, and she settled into comfort. Pulling her closer, I brought her back to meet my chest and made lazy circles on her stomach.

"I love you," I said, placing a kiss on the back of her head. When I remembered my mission for this afternoon, I groaned.

"I didn't think it was that bad," she joked sarcastically.

"My parents are hosting a party in two weeks. Wait a second," I laughed, catching what she said. "*That bad?* Guess I'll have to try harder next time." She squirmed under me when I pinched her nipple. "Anyhow, will you be my date? To my parents' party thing."

"We just made us a thing. Now you're talking about parents. I'm freaking out a little over here."

"It's just some party they throw every year. There's going to be close to seventy people there, not just my parents. Besides, you've already met my mom." I left out the choice words my mom had regarding Daisy that night at First Fridays. What my parents thought of her didn't matter, because I knew who she was.

"I guess I better go shopping for a tweed skirt suit," she sighed.

"Please, and I mean this with all my heart, do no such thing."

thirty-one
daisy

"THIS IS RIDICULOUS." I shook my head at the reflection in the mirror. Against Reid's wishes, I ran out and found a sage green tweed skirt and jacket suit. Paired with a modest kitty heel, I looked absolutely stuck up, nose in the air, *I don't tip more than ten percent*, hoity toity. It was perfect.

"Daze?" Reid called, his footsteps neared but abruptly stopped once he reached the doorway. "Are you ready? What in the world are you wearing?" he asked, taking me in.

"You like?" I asked, twirling and ending with a flick of the heel.

"I hate it," he laughed. "Don't get me wrong, you look incredible as always, but this isn't you. What about that cool pink lacey skirt thing or the purple and green sleeve-y thing?"

Despite his less than accurate descriptions, I knew exactly what he was talking about. Dang it, he was right. Those were magnificent pieces, and I pulled them off.

"Aren't you worried about your parents liking me?"

"No," he shrugged. "Anyone who can't see how amazing you are doesn't deserve to be in my life. I want you to be yourself. Please change."

My chest warmed. There he was, being all supportive again. My heart did a little thumpity thump and I knew I made the right choice trusting him to be my first official boyfriend. *That's right. I had a boyfriend.*

"I love you," I said with a smile.

Bringing his hand to his heart, he mimicked being shot by Cupid's arrow. "Ah, I'll never tire of hearing that."

An hour later, Reid's sports car hummed down the road. The Flores residence looked just as I imagined it would. Surrounded by a vast and perfectly manicured lawn, a decorated two-story colonial stood. Meticulously trimmed trees framed the entrance, shaped in climbing spirals. Squared bushes lined the front beneath rows of windows.

Music carried through the house mixed with light chatter. Steadying myself, I took a deep breath. I didn't remember being this nervous since my last first day of school. Approval from others hadn't mattered much since then, but this time it did.

I hated it.

Reid's warmth spread through my fingers, up my arm, when he laced his fingers in mine. The connection grounded me and having him made this feeling worth it.

We followed the music, hand in hand, to the backyard. A band played on top of a stage that had been built towards the back of the yard. The color changing leaves created a colorful canvas that was the perfect backdrop for the evening. Lights were strung overhead, and servers walked around carrying trays of champaign and hor d'oeuvres.

The woman I recognized as Reid's mom spoke to a couple. A tall man stood next to her; his thick, dark hair was graying, as was his trimmed beard. His demeanor was confident, and he stood tall, commanding attention.

"Mom, Dad," Reid called to his mom and the salt and peppered man.

"Reid, darling," his mom crooned, embracing him with a peck on each cheek. His dad simply greeted him by name and a firm handshake and despite never having met him, I had a feeling that was the extent of affection his father ever showed him.

"Mom, you remember Daisy," Reid introduced me, reintroducing his mom, Carrey, and introducing his dad, Clinton. His hand rested on the small of my back as he stood strong next to me. "Daisy is my girlfriend."

"Lovely," Carrey overtly lied, pursing her lips. I pretended to not notice the widening of her eyes just as I pretended not to hear Clinton's scoff.

"Your home is incredible. Thank you for having me," I offered. Suddenly, I wished I had gone with the green suit instead of the lacy layered black dress and purple and green bell sleeve wrap.

I zoned out as they carried on in mundane conversation. When they parted to speak with other guests, Reid led me around, introducing me to each person we encountered. And each time he called me his girlfriend, I did my best to not read into the stares or full-body scans. I ignored when eyes locked on my pink streaked hair, or my free-flowing dress. In the face of perfect manicures, face lifts, suits and ties, I tended to stay self-assured, but here, I couldn't help but feel inferior.

It was like they knew my life-story with one look and judged me for it. They labeled me immediately as "not good enough." They only saw my circumstances. But I could endure a few hours of this if it meant having Reid. I knew he didn't see those things when he looked at me. Instead, he made me feel like I had put the stars in the sky and the fish in the sea.

Focused on keeping a light smile on my face, I nodded at each introduction without retaining a single name. Finally, Reid led me away, and I chugged a glass of water.

"Baby, be careful. You'll drown yourself," Reid laughed.

Air escaped my lungs as I took a deep breath. The feeling of being judged and caring that I was being judged created a panic in me. Unfamiliar with the feeling, the panic grew, and my palms began to sweat.

"Sorry, just a little nervous is all," I said, wiping my hands on my dress. "Um, restroom?"

"Down the hall to the right of the kitchen. Want me to show you?"

"No, no, I can manage."

His hand wrapped around my waist as I started walking away. "You're doing great, by the way. Please don't be nervous. You're the most interesting, cool, and gorgeous woman here."

Blushing, I walked briskly into the house. *Did he say to the right of the kitchen or right next to the kitchen?* Peeking around a corner, a hushed voice caught my ear.

"Did you see who he brought?" one woman asked quietly.

"Please, she's just the girl from that pottery place. He'll see she's not worth his time soon enough," the other woman said. Her voice was like nails on a chalkboard, and I immediately recognized her as the *I spill wine on purpose so I can feel bigger than service workers* woman—Liz.

The first woman hummed, "I don't know, they looked pretty locked in. Did you see the pink in her hair? Hello, seventh grade called. It wants its trashy highlights back."

Liz snickered. "He can try breaking up with me all he wants. Regardless, we're practically engaged. This is just commitment jitters, cold feet. Once the ring is on my finger, it won't really matter."

Bile rolled in my stomach. She still thought they were engaged or going to be engaged. What did that mean? Did Reid not tell her? Full bladder forgotten, I rushed to find my boyfriend.

thirty-two

reid

"I'M TELLING YOU, SON, Turbo is the company to invest in," Bob Dickover was still droning on about his latest investment. I looked over his shoulder towards the house, hoping to see Daisy return. It had been the longest five minutes of my life, listening to Bob. "A little birdie told me they're about to bring on some solar big wig in a new sustainable electrical power role—it's going to make the price skyrocket."

"Isn't that insider trading?" I asked, even though I knew the answer. I knew this sleazeball was up to no good.

Bob just let out a hearty laugh and said some bullshit about how the rich stay rich. Thankfully, Daisy's ethereal figure emerged from the house. With a wave, I caught her attention, and damn if watching her walk towards me didn't knock the air right out of my lungs. Goosebumps pricked my arms as she approached, and I didn't think I'd ever get used to the feeling. My body responded to her in ways it never did to others.

"Hey, can I talk to you for a minute?" she asked in a hushed tone as she approached. Those words always ignited an instant reaction of *oh shit*. And this was no different. And the fact that it was Daisy saying those words, my heart started beating double time.

Did something happen while she was inside? Did my mom say something to her? Oh no, did my dad say something to her? My thoughts were interrupted by my dad's voice booming through the speakers. "Can I have everyone's attention, please?"

Standing at the microphone stand, both his hands propped on his hips, he was a commanding figure. Knowing this was his annual address to compliment all the other board members and stroke his own ego, I was more than happy to run away with my girlfriend. Motioning my head to the house, I started drawing her away until a heavy hand on my shoulder drew me back.

"Son," *I wished he would stop calling me that.* "I think you should stay for this," Bob directed.

Daisy and I shared an inquisitive look and turned to face the stage.

"Thank you all for being here tonight," my dad opened his speech. "This is usually the part of the night where I talk about how amazing we all are at our jobs and making money," everyone laughed, raising their glasses. "Tonight, though, we have a special announcement. Tonight is a joyous occasion for our family, and we couldn't think of a better night to celebrate than here with all of you. Reid?"

At the call of my name, Bob hooted, directing attention to us and pointing at me.

"Most of you know my son, Reid," dad motioned to me in the crowd. "Raising him has been one of mine and Carrey's greatest accomplishments. He is smart and successful, and tonight, I have the pleasure of announcing his engagement to Elizabeth Dickover."

Hollers and whoops rose into the air and people began clinking their champagne glasses. I was taken aback by such a powerful reaction that my breath instantly got stuck in my throat and a knot formed in my stomach. Daisy was so shocked that her jaw almost touched the floor, and she looked to be on the brink of puking.

"Best get up there, son," Bob said, giving me a little push. I jerked my shoulder back, shoving his hand away.

Dazed, I walked to the stage, contemplating my next move. The crowd parted and the sea of people gave me supportive and celebratory words, with the occasional cheerful slap on my back. I wanted to tell them all to shut up and that none of this was real. I wanted to turn around, grab Daisy by the hand, and get the fuck away from all these phonies. But, here I was again, following the call of my father.

As I took my place on stage, I looked at him standing next to me. My father. The man who claimed to be a family man, who claimed to raise me and have it be his shining accomplishment. Instead, I knew it was between my mom and whatever nanny was hired for the week that taught me anything. Even then, I wondered if I was raised or molded. Molded to be who they wanted. Who they needed.

From the stage, I watched Daisy move towards the back of the crowd. *Stop her. Hold her until I get there. Daisy, please don't go.* I wanted to scream those words, yell at the people in the back and command them to stop her, but the words got caught in my throat.

"Speech!" Bob shouted, starting a chant.

"Dad, I told you I wasn't going to do this," I said out the side of my mouth.

He embraced me in a hug and patted my back, speaking into my ear. "I trust you to do what's best for the family."

Taking the microphone from him, I cleared my throat. I waited for the crescendo. For the director to lead me to the turning point, tell me what to do next so we can have our happy ending and roll credits. But no one was going to tell me what to do, and hell, wasn't that what I had wanted all along? It was my moment to stand on my own. Stand in conviction of who I wanted to be.

"Uh, hm, hello," I started, gathering my thoughts. "I wouldn't be who I am today without my parents. They dedicated their lives to guiding me to be the man who stands before you today. In that time,

I've learned many lessons. Most recently, they've taught me a great lesson in family, loyalty, and trust."

I was staring my dad directly in the eyes. His throat moved as he gulped, listening to my words.

"It is because of that lesson I have the unfortunate role of sharing that Liz and I are not engaged, nor will be engaged. We've gone our separate ways and I apologize for this spectacle. Please, enjoy the rest of your evening."

Heavy silence hung in the air. A collective gasp rose from a small section of the crowd at the sudden sound of the breaking of glass. My dad had already made his way offstage. Standing next to my mom, both their faces were crimson. Funnily, I realized I didn't care. They put themselves in this situation. They forced my hand.

Maybe they'd finally realize they couldn't control me any longer.

Approaching them, a scene played out of the corner of my eye. Elain Dickover attended to her husband's bleeding hand, calling for a doctor. So dramatic, this bunch. Liz stood next to her mother, but instead of tending to her father, her eyes met mine. I swore I could see the bright red laser beams shooting from them, aimed right at my chest.

"Do you have any idea what you have just done?" dad asked, furious. I shook my arm from the grip he gave me as soon as I was within distance.

"I'm very aware of what I just did, father. I am your son, not your scapegoat. I will not bind myself to a life of unhappiness to pay for your sins. Next time, you could, I don't know, keep it in your pants?"

Surprising me, dad swung for me just as mom chastised me, calling my name in a rough but hushed tone. I took a giant step back, missing my dad's fist. It took every ounce of control in my body to shove my hands in my pockets. I didn't want this. I didn't want to fight, verbally or physically. I just wanted my parents to love me through the life I wanted to live for myself.

"You ungrateful fuck." Dad spat the words out as mom looked around anxiously. Even in that moment, she was more concerned that others would see what was unfolding, tarnishing their image, rather than her husband trying to knock out her son.

Shaking my head, I scraped my jaw with my hand. "I'm going to walk away, because despite you showing me time and time again that you don't actually care about me, I still care about you." Dad gave a bitter laugh at that, and tears now threatened to fall from mom's eyes.

Turning to look at her, I take her hands in mine. "Mom, you deserve better. I hope the news does come out and you get out and finally live your life for yourself," I said, giving her a kiss on the forehead. "Now, if you'll excuse me, I have to go find the woman I love and explain away this entire situation."

The drive back to Daisy's was agonizing. Unsure of how she got home, I worried about her safety and what she was thinking. Surely, she knew I wasn't actually engaged. I could only hope she believed and trusted in how I felt about her.

My foot was heavy on the pedal as I sped home on the back roads. Regardless of my speed, it wasn't fast enough. My sweaty palms gripped the wheel while my heart beat so hard, the sound traveled to my ears. When flashing red and blue appeared in my rearview mirror, I slammed my fist on the steering wheel in anger.

Begrudgingly, I pulled over and rolled down my window. "License and registration," the cop demanded from outside my opened window.

Straining my neck, I looked to see the officer's name badge. LAW-SON.

"Kendrick?" I asked.

"Reid? Hey man, nice ride. When did you get this?" he asked, slapping the hood of my sports car and leaning down to meet my eye.

"A few months ago," I answered shortly. Daisy was on my mind. I had to get to her. "Listen, I'm on my way to Daisy. I really need to see her."

"Daisy? Is she okay? Is it Carl?" he shot off rapid-fire questions, his authoritative voice taking over.

"No, it's not Carl. Something stupid happened and I just need to talk to her and explain things."

He chewed his lip in a way that I hoped meant he was contemplating letting me go. "I understand, man, but you were going seventeen over the limit. I gotta ticket you."

Swearing under my breath, I opened my wallet, handed him my license, and dug my registration from the depths of my glove box.

Hanging my head, I waited for him to return. Self-pity took over as all the times I chose to play into other people's plans for me over my own desires replayed in my head. I'd waited too long, wasted too many years. I was just over thirty and this was where it left me—possibly having lost my first love. My first real, bones deep, love.

"Here you go," Kendrick returned to my car, handing me my license, registration, and a printed-out sheet. "Sorry, man, just doing my job. Next time–"

The chatter of his radio cut him off. As he focused on the words coming through the piece of equipment on his chest, I watched his face drop and all the color drain away. Static clouded the voice on the other end of the radio.

"We *have a 3503 at a business residence, Slay and Clay.*"

thirty-three
daisy

My stomach roiled as I charged out of the house. I had to find Reid and get the hell out of the godforsaken party filled with god-forsaken people. Thanks to his tall figure, I spotted him easily. An animated stocky man was alternating between talking to him and slapping him on the shoulder.

Forgetting my manners, I breezed past the man without an introduction. "Hey, can I talk to you for a minute?" I asked Reid quietly.

Concern passed behind his eyes. Just as he opened his mouth to speak, his father's voice carried through the speakers, cutting him off. "Can I have everyone's attention, please?"

Reid looked back at the stage where his dad stood. When he turned back to face me, I pleaded with my eyes. Thankfully, he understood the meaning. Willing the hor d'oeuvre's to stay in my stomach, and not splattered all over the overpriced glass platform, relief washed through me as he inclined his head towards the house.

We stopped abruptly when Reid froze, the stocky man saying something to him.

"Thank you all for being here tonight," Clinton started. "This is usually the part of the night where I talk about how amazing we all are at our jobs and making money." *Ugh. Gross.* "Tonight, though, we have a special announcement. Tonight is a joyous occasion for our family, and we couldn't think of a better night to celebrate than here with all of you. Reid?"

The man who gave me total creep vibes hollered and pointed to Reid. A figure approached my side. Out of the corner of my eye, I found Liz had joined us. I balled my fists, trying to hold my nervous and frustrated energy in.

"Most of you know my son, Reid," Clinton continued. "Raising him has been one of mine and Carrey's greatest accomplishments. He is smart and successful, and tonight, I have the pleasure of announcing his engagement to Elizabeth Dickover."

Did he just say "engagement?" As in, Reid and Liz are engaged? My stomach lurched and I stared at Reid, my mouth agape. He looked just as shocked as me. I knew it had to be a lie.

"Best get up there, son." The man, who I now figured was Liz's dad, tried giving Reid a push towards the stage, but I saw his anger that simmered beneath the surface. Liz grabbed onto her father's arm, placing a kiss on his cheek.

Frozen in place, I watched him as he walked to the stage. "There he goes, my fiancé." A scratchy voice whispered into my ear. *Liz.*

"Bless your heart, sweetie," I said amiably, turning to face her. "He's not your fiancé. He's not your anything."

"Try again," she said in her cringe inducing way. I followed her gaze and we watched as Reid stood next to his father, the party guests cheering. "You see? He's gone up there to give his engagement speech. He may have warmed your bed for a night, but he's going to build a home with me. Your presence is no longer required. You are dismissed."

The look of superiority on her face was enraging. And so misplaced. I knew Reid, and I knew there was no way in hell he was going to go along with the engagement. But then again, I also knew he went along with it before for the sake of his family. Who was to say he wouldn't do it again?

My chest tightened and the air grew thick. I took a deep breath, clutching my chest. Regardless of what the truth was, I had to get out of there. Colliding shoulders with Liz, I beelined for the exit.

"Speech!" Liz's father shouted, inciting chants from the others. I didn't bother to turn around, see if Reid was going through with a speech. Instead, I reached the path lined with greenery that led to the front when a voice called after me.

"Daisy, darling," Carrey called. Turning to face her, I hoped for some words of encouragement or reassurance. "I am so sorry, dear. Reid has to do what is best for the family. We never intended for anyone else to be caught in the crosshairs. I wish you all the happiness."

I could feel the sadness in my eyes, and in my heart, as I looked at her. It had always been a dream of mine to have a partner whose mother could stand in for mine, one that would welcome me with open arms. Many daydreams of mine were filled with getting manicures together, going to lunch, and baking holiday cakes. Obviously, this would never be that, and that sunk my heart and hopes.

This was why I didn't do relationships. We should have never labeled the damn thing.

"My mother was never particularly good at caring for me, so I've grown to recognize a genuine family when I see one. Reid loves you so much." Tears now slid down my cheek. "He loves you so much, and I'm telling you right now that if you continue to push this engagement on him, you will lose him. Probably forever."

My whole life, I had experienced disappointment. Disappointment at never knowing my father. Disappointment at my mother not being able to put me first. Disappointment when I opened the door to another questionably stained motel room. When I created this new life for myself, I made it so I couldn't experience disappointment at the hand of another person ever again.

Yet, it happened. Reid snuck in when I left the door to my heart cracked. Then, when I noticed he was there, I let him stay. Even going as far as to roll out the welcome mat. I knew this was the risk, but I thought it was worth it if it meant I could have Reid.

But as I waited for the Uber I called, because I didn't want to have to explain the situation to a friend, I couldn't help but wonder...*was it really worth it?*

Pulling up outside the storefront, I noticed Polly speaking with Geraldine, looking over one of Geraldines piece's she had up for sale. I slapped a smile on my face as I entered. The bell I typically found cheery grated against my frustration, and Polly and Geraldine turned to greet me.

"Hey there boss," Polly greeted in her typical joyful tone. "Where's hot stuff?"

Geraldine's eyes lit up. "Oh, who's hot stuff?"

"Reid Flores." Polly responded, meeting Geraldine's excitement with her own.

"Clinton and Carrey's boy? How wonderful!"

I weakly smiled at Geraldine's comments. "Yeah, well, I'm not sure there's anything there to boast about. A thing," I waved my hand, expelling the topic away, "happened."

Polly and Geraldine shared a looked, but thankfully dropped it. "Well, I know Kendrick didn't work out. So, if you're back on the market, my son is still single." Turning to Polly, Geraldine explained.

"Dane has been hopelessly in love with Thalia for years. When she married Marc, Dane picked up and moved to Vermont. I'm trying to get him to move back, and I'm sure he would for our Daisy here."

"Thalia is Theo's sister. You may have met her at First Fridays. Theo is engaged to my best friend, Ellie." I explained to Polly, and she nodded in understanding. I laughed as Geraldine gave me a hug, putting her arm around my back and squeezing my side. "I'll be sure to remember-"

We turned in unison to look at the entrance as the bell above the door rang. A greasy man entered, and anger danced behind his eyes. *Carl.* Polly and Geraldine must've sensed the danger as we all tensed together.

"Hello sir," Polly greeted more kindly than warranted, given the hatred that radiated off him. "Can I help you?"

His eyes zeroed in on me as he realized my presence. Pulling the corners of his mouth up, his face transformed into a sickly smile. "I'm here for her." His voice was harsh, and I knew Polly recognized the voice when she gave me a sidelong look. Discreetly, I nodded, signaling to her that we needed to get away. Geraldine, the smart as a whip woman she was, and having attended many trainings and lectures at the station, caught the silent conversation as well.

Carl's hand, fingernails caked in dirt and all, slowly moved behind his back. I didn't want to venture a guess as to what he was reaching to, but I had a good idea.

Grabbing a vase on the stand next to me—Geraldine's vase—I chucked it, aiming for his big, stupid head. "Run!" I yelled, chucking the next piece of pottery I could grab. I could see Polly contemplating her next move, reaching for something to throw herself. Forcefully, I gave her a shove towards the door. "Go!"

Carl stumbled back as the pieces made contact with his pudgy, but solid, body.

"You fuckin' bitch," he grunted, picking himself up off the ground. "I told you I was gonna get ya,' and I always make good on my promises. Or don't yous' remember the pretty little coma I put your ungrateful ass in?"

I watched as Polly and Geraldine ran through the door to the throwing room. At least they could get to safety through the back door. With a menacing gesture, Carl's hand shone brightly as he displayed a gun. It felt as if my heart was beating in my throat from the spike of adrenaline the sight gave me. *Think Daisy. Think.*

I had to move before he could get the gun in position, and I sure as hell didn't want to be stuck between him and the shelves when he did. Before he could disengage the safety, I charged at him, swinging a chair towards his figure.

The gun slid across the floor, landing in front of the doorway to the throwing room. I made a run for the front door and cursed when I noticed the debris lying on the floor, blocking the path needed to open the door wide enough to squeeze through. Carl was already getting the gun in hand and I knew clearing the debris would waste too many precious seconds. On a breath, I pivoted and ran up the apartment stairs.

A loud bang rang out just as I reached my door. Slamming the door shut, I engaged the deadbolt and shoved my door security bar under the handle. Ellie had bought it for me when she saw the room I rented in the big house. She said a girl could never be too cautious. Thank goodness for my best friend.

Finally taking a breath, shivers went through my body, knowing that Carl had control of the gun again.

thirty-four

reid

"10-4 Officer Lawson responding, four minutes out," Kendrick called back on his radio. "Follow me."

He didn't need to explain further. I was going to follow regardless of if he wanted me to or not. Daisy was in danger, and it would take more than the law to keep me away.

We zipped around the curve of the road, approaching speeds of twenty-five, thirty over. Main street was thinning out as night began taking over and thankfully we barreled through quickly.

As unbelievable as what was in front of me was, I had seen it before. I had walked over broken glass covering the ground. I had assessed a broken shop window. Only this time, it was the window we'd only just replaced, and my chest ached with pain from the fear that iced my veins. The only sound coming from the dark space was an aggressive pounding.

"Open up, bitch," Carl's gruff voice yelled angrily. I recognized his familiar disdain laced words from the hundreds of messages he'd left the weeks prior. "I brought you a gift. Givin' you what yous deserve."

An arm tugged me back as I launched towards the busted window. "Reid, stand back. That's an order," Kendrick barked at me.

I paused at the window and peered in. At the top of the stairs, a stocky, disheveled man pounded on the door. An object in his hand glinted and fear iced my veins.

"He has a fucking gun," I quietly exclaimed.

Cursing, Kendrick called back over the radio. "This is Officer Lawson responding to the 3503 at Slay and Clay. Back-up needed. Suspect is armed and attempting to enter a private residence above business."

The sound of wood snapping and a door slamming cracked through the air. Darkness closed around my vision, and I charged into the building, ignoring Kendrick's calls. Unfazed by the broken chairs and shards of pottery, I bolted for the stairs. Taking the stairs two at a time, I took in the broken door hanging off its hinges.

Daisy's grunts mingled with the mans, and I moved on autopilot. Shuffling could be heard throughout the apartment and the crash of a vase. The living room was in disarray, her funky, weird-ass lumpy lamp was on its side, the couch shoved feet in the opposite direction. A scream pierced the air. My head snapped toward the shriek and I charged into the bedroom.

The gruff man covered Daisy with his body. They grappled on top of her bed, getting caught up in the comforter and pillows. She was putting up a fight, fists flying. With a whack, she caught him in the jaw. *That's my girl.*

He pulled his hand back, preparing to strike her back, and the weapon caught my eye again. Lunging, I grabbed his arm. He howled in pain as I brought his arm back, locking it in position behind him. Swinging my free arm around his neck, I pulled him into a chokehold until he freed Daisy.

Scrambling away, she landed on the other side of the bed. Relief washed over me, knowing she was safe. Releasing Carl, he swung around to face me. Swiftly, I struck the side of his neck with a knife-hand movement. With a pained grunt, he grabbed at the sore spot I had struck. He stumbled off the bed, attempting to charge towards me.

I pulled back, and with all the force I could muster, I roundhouse kicked him on the side of his face. The snap of his head was quick as he fell back.

Reaching my hand over the bed, I motioned for Daisy to come to me. Tears streaked her face as she collapsed into my chest. My heart thumped powerfully at the thought that I almost lost her, and at the thought that I didn't. Leading her out, I kept her close to me, encapsuled in my embrace.

Our story hung between us, the words we hadn't had the chance to say to each other. Instead, we held on to the other as we kept each other tethered to the Earth after what had happened. She gripped my arm with force, and in place of pain from her digging fingers, I felt comfort knowing she found in me what I found in her. Security.

"Police!" Kendrick and two other officers called. Guns drawn, they entered the apartment. Having taken in the scene, they rounded the corner of the hallway that led to the bedroom with determination. "Thank god," Kendrick sighed the moment he observed us.

"He's back there." The motion of my head directed them down the hall. Daisy stayed silent and glued to my side. Gingerly, I led her through her living room.

"Holy shit, is he alive?" one officer in the bedroom asked in disbelief.

"Got a pulse," another officer said. "Damn, they really did a number on him."

A small whimper escaped Daisy as she paused, taking in the disheveled space. "It's okay, baby. You're okay." I whispered into her ear while I stroked the side of her head.

Unwilling to let Daisy go, I held her close as I led her downstairs and on to the sidewalk, where we sat side by side. I was unsure how much time passed as I twirled a strand of her hair around my finger mindlessly. We watched silently as Carl was carted out on a flat board and loaded into the back of an ambulance. Happiness and vengeance enveloped me, knowing he couldn't hurt Daisy anymore.

"Daisy!" We looked up together to see Polly and Geraldine running towards us, each wrapped in a thin fleece blanket. "Oh Daisy," Polly dropped to her knees, pulling Daisy into her arms. "You stupid, stubborn woman," she cried. "Never do that again! We expected you to be right behind us. When you didn't follow—we—we heard..." Polly's voice trailed off she gasped for air from a sob.

Geraldine kneeled slowly, her knees cracking as she took her place with Polly and Daisy. "We heard the gunshot, Daisy. We were so scared something happened to you."

Daisy wiped at her wet cheeks and smiled brightly at her friends. "I'm okay." The three of them held onto each other, taking turns laughing and crying.

"Ladies," Officer Kelly interrupted gently. "I need to grab statements from everyone. Geraldine, why don't we start with you?"

Geraldine stood with a helping hand and walked off with Officer Kelly. Polly wiped away at her tears before giving Daisy one more squeeze. Looking between us, Polly sighed. "I'm going to give Poppy a call." With a small smile, she left Daisy and me alone.

"So, are you a secret ninja or something?" Daisy asked, squinting at me in suspicion. Her eyes were red rimmed and slightly puffy, but she glowed with love. "Cause that's something you should disclose to your girlfriend."

"Girlfriend?" I asked hopefully.

"Well, yeah. You found me and Bruce Lee'd the shit out of my attacker. Polly may have been spot on calling me stubborn and stupid, but I know enough to know I have to keep a man like you around."

I laughed with relief and schooled my expression, trying to not be overzealous. "Didn't you know? You're dating a former Taekwondo Pennsylvania State Championship winner."

"You literally do everything. It's annoying," she shook her head.

Guiding her face to mine, I claimed her with a kiss. Both our bodies sagged with content at the contact. I smiled against her lips as another voice called out her name. Ellie was yelling for her, calling her name a block away, as she sprinted towards us.

I chuckled and gave Daisy another quick kiss. "You are so loved."

Epilogue

one year later

Daisy

"I SHOULD'VE PACKED DIAPERS," I said, bouncing with excitement. "I think I might pee myself. Then you're going to be the weirdo dating the girl who peed herself."

"If you pee yourself, I will pee myself in solidarity," Reid said, slinging his arm over my shoulders.

The stage manager clapped his hands loudly, and in an authoritative voice called out. "It's time."

"Holy shit, it's time."

"It's time," Reid parroted, but with a much calmer demeanor. How could he be so blasé? Meanwhile, my body was threatening to vibrate itself into oblivion until it was nothing more than particles floating through the air. With a kiss on the temple, he gave my butt a pat and disappeared into the darkness backstage.

"You're a badass bitch. You're, like, so cool and awesome. You're going to do great." I chanted to myself softly with my eyes fixed on the ground. I felt a presence to my left and admired the bright pink and blue clogs that appeared next to my lavender platform heels.

"Cute shoes," I complimented. My voice was shaking, and anxiety was winning the war inside of me. Instead, I wanted to focus on something fun. Like cute shoes.

"Thanks," a smooth and confident voice said. "They're vintage." Looking up, I met my idol eye to eye. Macy Shivers. And holy moly, I was *definitely* going to pee myself.

"Ma-Macy Shivers," I stuttered. "Oh. My. God. You are my idol."

She laughed lightly as my jaw hung loose. Now *she* was, like, so cool and awesome. "And you're soon to be other aspiring artists' idol. How does it feel?"

It felt like a fever dream. That had to be it. I was in a dream. Carl actually shot me after all, and this was the afterlife. Or maybe he had put me in another coma, and I was laying in a hospital somewhere, spending my days dreaming. I had the man of my dreams. My mom was about to hit twelve months sober. Carl was sentenced to forty years in jail and would likely die there. And I was talking to Macy shittin' Shivers.

"Surreal." I blew a breath on the word.

The DJ on stage began his introduction, rattling off the long list of Macy's accolades.

We stared at the DJ as we stood off to the side, hidden by heavy black curtains. Macy spoke out the side of her mouth. "I've seen your work. It's inspired…"

"By you," I declared, cutting her off.

Smiling, she continued. "Nevertheless, it's gorgeous and you deserve this. My advice is to soak it up and never change. Know that being who you are is what got you here. With this comes expectations, and it's up to you to give those expectations a big middle finger."

A sharp laugh escaped me, accompanied by a small snort, and I slapped my hand to my mouth. How embarrassing. My idol was giving me advice and complementing me, and I snorted. *Snorted!*

"...Macy Shivers," the DJ announced.

Adjusting her shoulders, she straightened herself and stepped from behind the curtain onto the stage. Applause filled the stadium as she waved to the crowd. Taking her place behind the podium, she began her speech.

"Fifteen years ago, to this day, I was in this exact spot. Shaking in my dazzling styled shoes, I had no idea that a lifetime of creating, learning, and incredible experiences lay ahead of me. Today, I am so honored to present this year's Upcoming Ceramics Artist of the Year.

"The winner of this award exemplifies originality, tenacity, and craft.

"For eleven years, I've been on the board of judges for this award. For eleven years we've seen contestants write essays, send videos begging to win, and stalk us on social media. I've even been gifted a Louis Vuitton bag—which I vehemently declined, despite really wanting to keep it." She paused for the audience's laughter.

"But this was the first year we received a submission from someone who was not the artist in question."

Macy stepped to the side as a large screen dropped slowly from the ceiling. Reid's face lit up the screen, and my heart skipped several beats at his glowing smile. Tears brimmed my eyes as I was overcome with adoration. My man not only believed in me, but believed in me so much he took a step for me I'd been too scared to take myself. Looking out to the crowd, I found Reid, Ellie, Theo, my mom, Calley, and Polly.

Over the last year Polly had not only become my star employee but also my partner in the studio. The success I found as my business continued to grow became too much to handle. When my classes and student commission work were featured in a home and garden magazine, we were immediately booked out for six months. With the boom in growth, I needed someone to help run things so we could expand hours and manage the higher volume.

I was more than happy to ask Polly to do me the honor of becoming my partner.

Carl's attack on me was a wake-up call for my mom. She decided that day to join Alcoholics Anonymous, and she's stuck with it for a year. After her first sponsor moved across the country, Polly then stepped in as her sponsor. Polly was practically part of the family now—Reid and I even helped her move her daughter into her college dorm.

Thanks to Polly, my mom was a year clean and has held the same job for eight months. She saved every penny and moved from my couch into a room in the rooming house I first moved into when I first came to Chestnut Hills.

The smile on Reid's face as he looked up at the screen lit up my heart, and the tears streaming down my mom's face made me swell with pride.

"Hello," Reid on the screen cleared his throat. "My name is Reid Flores, and this is my submission for Daisy Bloom to be considered for the Upcoming Ceramics Artist of the Year award. Ceramics is her passion, and it shines not only through her work but also through how she supports other's work."

On the screen, we watched as Reid gave a tour of my studio. Pausing at each piece I'd created, he carefully took a panoramic shot, being sure to catch each angle. While walking between pieces, he explained how I taught classes, did community outreach, and commissioned my students' pieces. He ended on the finished product of *Dark Parts*

Bloom. I mimed clenching my heart as he explained my inspiration for the piece, and all the intricate parts.

"So, that's Daisy Bloom, the best goddamn—sorry—artist I've ever seen. Her work speaks for itself, and I hope you see that too. I thank you for your consideration," Reid said to the screen as it faded to black. The screen retreated to the ceiling and Macy returned to her place at the podium.

"It is with great pleasure I introduce the Upcoming Ceramics Artist of the Year, Daisy Bloom," Macy called through the microphone. Applause erupted as she motioned for me to join her on stage.

Lights blurred my vision, and I prayed I wouldn't trip as I walked across the stage. Happily, I accepted my award and a hug from Macy. Taking my spot at the podium, I cleared my throat.

"Wow. I just got to hug Macy Shivers," I squeaked, getting a laugh from the crowd. I took this moment to catch my breath. "I started pottery eight years ago as a way to feel some semblance of control. Molding and manipulating the clay gave me a sense of purpose and renewed spirit. At the time, I had no idea my new passion would grow into owning my own studio, where I get to teach the love of creating and help others pursue their dreams.

"I thought I did it all in a way that made me independent—I showed myself I didn't need anyone but myself. Through this journey, though, I learned that the people in my life made my success possible. Thank you to my best friend Ellie and her fiancé, Theo, for putting up with my weirdness, and helping me wrangle kids drinking clay water on their field trips. Thank you to Calley, my amazing employee and star athlete, and Polly, my new partner who taught me our past doesn't define us. Thank you to my beautiful mom for showing me what it means to be strong and resilient. And thank you to my incredible boyfriend, Reid, for supporting me, cheering me on from the sidelines, and encouraging me to be myself and claim my greatness."

My throat closed as I watched the people I loved cheer me on.

This was what it meant to have a family.

Reid

The quiet street settled my soul. I soaked in the peaceful walk to Meryl's Makes & Bakes. Light dew of the morning coated the shop windows, and a light breeze ruffled my hair.

After Daisy's award ceremony last night, we surprised her with a party at the shop. Every student, client, and friend showed up and showed out. The crowd was so large it spilled out onto the street. Even Mrs. Larkin showed up. A little slower and older, she was still walking with purpose and ferocity. Daisy sobbed so hard she had to reapply her mascara after crying it all off.

We gave Kendrick a heads up and the police were able to block off part of the street. Not that we needed it because the whole town was celebrating with us. There wasn't a car on the road.

I didn't know the pride I felt while looking at her was possible. My love for her grew every day and while it still scared me, I couldn't picture my life any other way.

When I saw my mom embrace her with a tight squeeze, and Daisy accepted her without a question, I was a goner.

Bob Dickover made good on his blackmail and revealed dad's affair to the board. At the end of the day, the board members didn't really care. They swept it under the rug and had a laugh at how it was good for the soul to have a little fun. Luckily, that was the last straw for mom. She filed for divorce the next morning.

Now, mom was happily a regular in my life and became good friends with Daisy.

"Good morning, Meryl," I called as I entered her small shop.

"Reid, baby, how're you?" she asked, tying off the pink bow.

I smiled at her. "Fantastic."

"Soon to be even better," she returned with a wink.

I took the box of treats she slid across the glass case and waited for her to finish making our iced lattes. Whistling, I walked back to the shop. I walked back home.

Daisy was sweeping when I returned, gathering the crumbs and popped balloons from the night before that littered the floor. She didn't hear me as I entered and set our coffees and treats on the table. Coming up behind her, I slid my hands around her waist and kissed her neck. The way she slacked against my touch would never get old.

"Come," I said, "I got us coffees and pastries."

"I need to clean," she said, giggling.

"Everyone is coming in an hour to help clean. Let's drink coffee and eat—for old times' sake." I tugged on her hand and pulled out a chair at one of the painting tables.

"Remember the first time we met?" I asked, while I untied the bow.

"When your ex broke a glass of wine, on purpose?"

"Right," I chuckled. That felt like a lifetime ago, one I never wanted to go back to. "Okay, then, the second time we met?"

She hummed while sipping her coffee. "I wanted to snap your head off for questioning me after I was robbed."

"And I sweetened you up with this exact meal. You played right into my hands. Like putty."

She gasped and laughed at that. "Sure, babe. Whatever helps you sleep at night."

Her smile transformed into full shock as she took in the pastry box I pushed in front of her.

In the box laid twelve perfect mini chocolate eclairs. In the center, in pink icing, the eclairs read MARRY ME? I shifted out of the chair and onto one knee, pulling out the velvety pink ring box.

"Hell yeah!" she shouted and tackled me to the ground. In a fit of laughter, she covered me with kisses.

Happily, I placed the ring on her finger.

"So, they'll be here in an hour, huh?" she asked. When I nodded, she looked back at the stairs to the apartment. "Care to celebrate?"

Gripping her ass, I moved to carry her across the messy space and up the stairs.

"With you? Always."

Acknowledgements

WRITING MY FIRST BOOK took two years, writing my second took a few months. With each finished project, the easier it gets, and that is thanks to all the support from the people around me.

When my first book was finally published, the outpouring of love from my husband, C, and my sisters, J, A, and R, kept me motivated to keep going. They were the ones that pushed me, and affirmed me every step of the way that what I was doing mattered. Without them, these ideas would have stayed in my head.

For this book in particular, they inspired the village of Chestnut Hills. In the same way the community came together to help Daisy rebuild, my husband and sisters have done the same for me. After an extremely difficult time in my life, they came in to pick up the pieces. I could've done it alone, but I didn't have to. In fact, they wouldn't let me.

If I could have one wish granted, it would be that everyone is blessed with such a strong community as I have been.

I also want to thank my best friend, A, who listened to me talk about my journey and accepted that I wouldn't share any of my goals for fear of failure. Instead, she sat silently, held space for me, and let me succeed on my own. Thank you for being exactly who I needed.

My heart belongs to my readers and reviewers. Thank you so much for allowing me to tell you a story, a story that I love. The words you leave me when you tell me what my story meant to you bring me so much light. I cannot quantify the amount of tears I've cried over your praise.

Lastly, I want to thank myself. This is my second book, and I'm poised to complete my third (keep reading for a sneak peek), and I am proud of myself for accomplishing what I have so far.

In the words of goddess Illona Maher:

> It's okay to be proud of what you've done, and it's okay to believe you deserve something because you've put in the work for it.

Not ready to leave Chestnut Hills? Want to meet Thalia's baby?

Keep reading for a special preview of Maria Rosewood's next novel

Between the Hydrangeas

Coming soon

prologue
dane

"Yello'," I harrumphed through my car's speakerphone.

"Purple!" my childhood best friend greeted with our standard color exchange, her giggle carrying through the open space of my car. "Hey grumpy pants. What cha' doing?"

Looking ahead, I cruised steadily down the sparse winding road. "Driving. You?"

"Same. Just headed home, wondering what kind of bargain I have to make with whom to get this baby out of me."

I snorted lightly. "Yeah? How much longer do you have?"

"Well, I'm not due for two more weeks, but I've been cramping all day. I've already stopped showing houses. I'm about to lose my ever loving mind sitting behind a desk all day, but even then, it's been hard to walk for more than ten minutes at a time."

"You make pregnancy sound like a dream."

She sighed on the other end, a sigh I had heard hundreds of times on our hundreds of calls. A sigh I hadn't heard in person in years. They said distance would make the heart grow fonder, but I was testing a theory that distance would make the heart forget.

"How's Marc?" I asked, feigning interest.

"He's alright. The commute for his new job has been taking a toll, but we're manage—oh, ow!" she yelped on the other end. The foreign and abrupt sound made my heart stop.

"Thalia? Thalia, what happened? Are you okay?"

Her breathing was ragged on the other end. "I—yeah—I think so. I think I just had a contraction."

"A contraction?! Where are you? How far are you from the hospital? Call 911!" I panicked. She laughed, and I cursed the aloofness of her spirit. "Thalia." I demanded roughly.

"It's fine. They won't admit me until my contractions are five minutes—ah!" she yelped again, breathing harshly for the longest minute of my life before cursing under her breath. "I—I think my water broke."

I felt the color drain from my face. I didn't know much about childbirth, but I knew enough that contractions that close together, and water breaking—whatever the hell that meant—was a sign of imminent baby birthing.

"Thalia, go. Drive to the nearest hospital." She cut me off with another scream. Her contractions couldn't have been more than four or five minutes apart. "I'll call Marc. Go!"

"Okay, tell him I'll be at Chestnut Hills Union Hospital—ah!"

I ended the call before she finished her yell and pulled over, frantically picking up my phone from the center console. Scrolling through my contacts, I made all the movements needed to call her husband clumsily. While I shook, listening to the blaring ringing, I typed a frantic text to her brother, Theo. Typos littered every other word as I tried to will my fingers steady.

Dane

> Thal ia labor chest nut hill union hospit

"Dane?" Marc answered with a question. We'd always been friendly enough, but I think he knew I was always pining after his wife. Even since we were kids, trading pudding cups at lunch.

"Marc, I was just on the phone with Thalia and she went into labor."

"What?!" His panic mirrored mine, which only made me panic more.

"Her contractions couldn't have been more than four minutes apart and she thinks that her water broke." The sound of his car accelerating could be heard through the receiver. "She's on her way to Chestnut Hills Union Hospital right now. I texted Theo."

"Can you text him and tell him I'm on the way? Tell Thalia too, let her know I love her, and will be there as fast as I can."

I swallowed the lump in my throat. "Sure thing, man. Drive safe."

"Hey, Dane?"

"Yeah?"

"Thank you." The line went dead before I could respond.

I sent the text to Thalia and Theo before pulling back onto the road.

Dane

Marc is on the way.

I typed out the next message, sighing before sending.

Dane

He said he loves you.